The Choice

The Choice

P.C.R. Penfold

AuthorHouse™
1663 Liberty Drive
Bloomington, IN 47403
www.authorhouse.com
Phone: 1-800-839-8640

Published by AuthorHouse 02/21/2013

ISBN: 978-1-4817-8422-1 (sc)
ISBN: 978-1-4817-8423-8 (e)

This book is printed on acid-free paper.

Chapter 1

Martha sat in the garden studying her toes, trying to decide whether burgundy or purple varnish would look best. As she had neither, it didn't really matter but it took her mind off other things and in particular, the extraordinary discovery of a past life her father had lived which was entirely unknown to her. Her dark hair swung forward and she lifted her face to the sun, sending her hair back into a shimmering moving curtain as she squinted up at the sky, absent-mindedly studying the pillowy shapes of the clouds. Her world was standing still at this moment; her father, with whom she had lived for all of her life, had died less than a month ago and this was the first opportunity she had found to be outside in her small garden. Seeing so many weeds, she wished she had started it the weekend before,

She sipped her coffee and idly watched the blue tits eating the bag of nuts she had put out for them, their colours brilliant in the sunshine. Temporarily caught in this peaceful bubble, it took her mind away from the strangely personal task of going through her father's papers which she had started that morning. It had naturally fallen to Martha to clear the accumulation of possessions reflecting his life but her father's papers had revealed a surprising story and right now, she was holding her secret close, almost afraid to return and discover more although she knew that was what she must do. Again lifting her face and closing her eyes, she felt the caress of a faint warm breeze and she treasured these moments of calm before collecting herself to go back and read the papers that she had not fully understood. She thought about contacting Calvin to come and help her but decided that what she had found was too personal and she needed to face it alone.

The trouble was, she thought, living in a small village sometimes felt as if other people knew more about her business than she did. And when it came to affairs of the heart, there were few secrets that could be safeguarded against the village gossipers. For instance, her relationship with Calvin was openly discussed now that her father had died, leaving her the physical presence of the house but not one person really close in whom she could confide. So the neighbours in their kindly but misguided way considered it was their duty to question her frequently on the plans and intentions of Calvin and herself despite the fact she was now twenty three years old and at the moment there was nothing she wanted to tell them.

Sighing heavily at the thought of the task ahead, she came back into the house, blinking against the sudden darkness after the sunshine, resolving this time to go through her father's wardrobe and desk thoroughly. She washed the dirt from the garden from her hands and made fresh coffee. Sitting at her father's desk she brushed aside her hair along with her aversions, and still feeling like an intruder, she turned over papers she had never seen before, even though most of them were the impersonal detritus of ever day life. There were utility bills mixed in with receipts for video recorder, radio, food mixer and other long since defunct appliances. The receipts and guarantees had outlived the machines by many years. Mixed in amongst these were birth, death and marriage certificates of people she had never known and these were the ones she had previously put on one side to study later along with some letters.

Individually they still told her very little, so she began putting them into piles with the same names next to each other. There were faded and creased letters as well as certificates which she still felt reluctant to look at, some sixth sense holding her back from reading or studying them more closely. Earlier that morning, she had cried over photos of her mother and father standing together, looking so young and vulnerable and laughing at the unknown photographer. She had smiled at photos of herself aged about six trying to ride a bicycle, the moment cleverly captured just before she fell, so clear she could almost remember the feeling of those perilous, wobbling moments. She put them all in a pile and still procrastinating, she stood at the wardrobe and started folding her father's clothes instead. She was reluctant to throw out even the most worn out of jumpers and trousers, wanting to defer such a final act in case she might regret having so little tangible evidence left of his life.

Since her mother's death when she was eight years old, she and her father had enjoyed a comfortable and unusually mature companionship. She had felt responsible for him and he for her, a more complete relationship than they might have had if her mother had lived or even if she had a brother or sister. Her father had continued to work at the architect's office in Maidstone, and her grandmother had looked after her after school with neighbours or parents of friends filling in the spaces. Holiday times had been more difficult but somehow they had managed and she had never felt neglected or pushed aside. She understood why the neighbours felt so responsible for her, she thought with a mixture of tolerance and irritation because they had always been there for her. But she wasn't a school child or even a teenager any longer. She was an attractive and independent young woman, although perhaps because she still lived at home with her father, the neighbours saw her differently. As an adult, they had both benefitted from the arrangement financially and so she had never seen any reason to live separately from her father. That had changed now, much quicker and sooner than she would have ever guessed and the void in her life was aching and painful.

It had been a difficult two months, her father was only in his sixties when he had been diagnosed with cancer of the liver and it had overtaken him very swiftly after that. She had wondered if he had been suffering for a lot longer and not telling her so that she wouldn't worry and now she would never know, could never ask him and she thought that sadly it wouldn't have changed the outcome. The doctor at the local village surgery had sent him for tests at the hospital two weeks after he had first complained of pains in his side. Cancer had been suspected right from the beginning and they were both waiting worriedly for the appointment for him to see the consultant who would then decide on the course of treatment he should have. But there hadn't been enough time because he had collapsed suddenly at work in great pain. The ambulance had rushed him off to hospital where he was given pain relieving drugs. When the news finally caught up with Martha that day at work, she had visited him that evening. Already the doctors she spoke to made it very clear that he was unlikely to recover. After that, she visited him every day hoping for an improvement, but after a week she knew they were right. She had been very angry at them for telling her, not wanting to hear such negative and pessimistic prognosis when she hadn't invited their opinion. But her anger hadn't helped and she could see a fateful acceptance in her father's eyes and in his tired gentleness towards her. She had wanted him to fight but instead, he was calm, complacent and accepting. She turned her frustrations against the doctors for being the ones to give up on him and for voicing what she now knew in her heart that he really was dying. But they were implacable, he was too weak, all they could do was ease the pain and all she could do after that was to be there for him, holding his hand in hers when he died two weeks later.

Looking at his clothes, she picked up a scarf and folded it, then felt its' softness against her cheek imagining the smell of his favourite soap still lingering there. She had given it to him for Christmas the year before and now she carefully placed it on the pile of clothing in front of her. She knew the time had come for her to be practical and not bitter at the suddenness of the past events, she needed to concentrate on all the legal matters in her father's desk. She would go through policies and bank statements, determined this time to open letters, read certificates and decide what she needed to keep and what she could throw away. She must also do her best to unravel the hidden stories in the papers she had seen earlier.

Methodically, she started with the certificates of the birth and death of her mother which were all as she would have expected to find. Next, she turned her attention to a packet of letters, some of which were written in French, a language she liked and had studied to a higher than ordinary school level. These were the ones which had been troubling her ever since this morning. She had opened the ones in English first and saw they were from her father to his mother about a woman called Marilor.

She felt ready to read them again in control now, of her initial feelings of shock and disbelief because the letters revealed that her father had been married before, many years before she was born. Carefully going through the certificates, they confirmed what she had read in the letters, that a marriage had taken place between her father Jeremiah Ballard and a French woman called Marilor Piske. The marriage certificate was dated May 1941 and had taken place in France. Now throwing papers around haphazardly, she searched frantically for a death certificate for Marilor but could not find one. Instead, she found a birth certificate for a baby girl born in December of that same year. The name on the certificate was Abigail Ballard, naming Marilor as the mother and Jeremiah as the father. Martha's searching suddenly stopped as she stared at it in astonishment and wished futilely that she could ask her father what had happened to these people. Was this baby girl really her half sister? Why had he never told her? Why had he taken these secrets to the grave?

Martha abandoned all the papers where they were. She needed to digest this and decided that a large brandy would help. Her father had never mentioned any connection with France, although she knew he could speak the language fluently, but these letters revealed a life she could never have guessed at. She was drawn magnetically back to the desk to find out more. The letters sent to his mother showed that he had spent several years in France as a youth, living and working on a farm where Marilor was evidently either a close neighbour or she had lived there too. In his letters he told his mother of his growing friendship with Marilor, a love that was developing despite their obvious youth. Too young to be conscripted in to the war effort when it started, apparently he was not too young to marry. As time went on, the letters told his mother in vague hints how he was helping in the resistance movement; nothing was very substantial, just saying he had met an English pilot and been able to direct him to a better hiding place in the German occupied area where he was living. He also wrote about his frustration at the lack of support he received from Marilor in his efforts to help his countrymen. His mother had evidently kept his letters to her but there were no letters from her to him and no apparent address either so Martha had to conclude that he had thrown these away after receiving them, if he ever did. The letters were now taking on a note of sadness and frustration as Jeremiah complained that his wife of so few months, even though she was now pregnant, had become much too friendly with a German Officer stationed near to her father's farm. Jeremiah suspected that she had caused the capture of some Englishmen before they could be safely returned to British shores. He suspected that the seemingly duplicitous Marilor had been passing on detailed information to her German friend of things she had found out and were spoken to her in confidence. It was increasingly clear from the anguished tone of the letters that he was devastated by all this and wanted to come home, with the intention of joining the forces when he could.

But what had happened to the baby Abigail? Martha had exhausted all the information available in the letters between her father and his mother and could find no more after 1941. She had to presume this may have been because he had indeed come back to England. Surely Marilor was not still alive, that would make her father a bigamist. She couldn't see him in that light at all. But did she, Martha, have a half sister living in France?

There was no-one she could ask. Her grandparents on both sides were now dead and until that moment she had not known that she might have another living relative. She searched for more letters, and found two more in a different hand and in French. These were from Marilor and were addressed to Jeremiah at her grandmother's house, both asking him to return, sounding anxious and accusing, but not loving. There was no mention of a baby in them. There was another letter in spidery writing from an aged aunt to Jeremiah, also written to him at his mother's address in England saying how sorry she was to hear about the traitorous acts of his wife and how sad she was, knowing they would never see Jeremiah's daughter Abigail. They were proud that he had come home to join the Air force and fight the enemy from England in this terrible war. This was dated June 1943.

Martha thought with some amazement, that 1941 must have been a momentous year for her father. He had married, had a child, joined the Air force and changed his country of residence all at the age of eighteen. Added to this, he had also discovered that his wife was a traitor. She sat for a long time, holding the letters and thinking back to uncover some hidden memory with which she could link the past to the present. How could her father have lived with such secrets all these years and told her nothing of this part of his life. Why ever hadn't she asked him about his past? She asked herself again, when it was all too late. She had assumed he had always lived in the village of Elmswood or Yalding where his mother had lived. Like many people of his age, she knew he was reluctant to speak about the War or his part in it and now she wondered if anyone else living knew about his past. Searching for more clues, she found the answer to one of the many questions buzzing in her head. Neatly folded and still in its envelope with a French stamp was a letter from a man signing himself Claude Rombouts. It stated very starkly, that after the arrest of Marilor and the trial which followed and which lead to her conviction and imprisonment as a collaborator during the war, Marilor had now died. The letter was dated February 1955. A prison term which had evidently lasted for at least ten years.

Martha still had one burning question unanswered in all this maze of paper. What had happened to Abigail? It felt to Martha as if this was her father's unfinished business as well as a possible living link to the past. She resolved to find out more. She felt ready now to call Calvin and tell him what she had uncovered and hope that he would understand that she had got to go to France and find out what had happened to her father in France and to Abigail. She felt she had no choice.

Chapter 2

Martha had been going out with Calvin for about six months. It was an easy going relationship and they were both quite happy with it, with no wish on either side to change anything. Calvin loved his motor bike which was really a hobby for him. He had been riding motor bikes since he was sixteen years old, progressing to larger and more expensive bikes until this most recent purchase of a Triumph Bonneville. He worked in the town planning department of a large council run office, checking drawings of traffic modifications and high street planning. He lived in the village next to Elmswood, where Martha lived, called Blackwater, with a young couple who had bought a house with a mortgage which stretched their budget, so they had invited Calvin to rent a room and share the kitchen and bathroom facilities. Calvin liked his independence and renting gave him a chance to save before taking on a mortgage himself. He was ambitious in a quiet non-spectacular way, studying to improve his position at work, saving to buy a flat or maybe a house. He was beginning to hope that his relationship with Martha would blossom and he had wanted to see more of her for a long time. He put his savings in the Building Society where she worked and had made a point of going to the counter where she was on duty on a regular basis. He had asked her out when she was closing her till one day ready for the lunch break, timing his invitation to give her very little chance to make an excuse not to join him for a cup of coffee.

Calvin's grandmother was from Jamaica and he worried that Martha might feel prejudiced towards him with his darker skin but she had never ever mentioned what his roots might have been, just shown interest when he told her and expressed the hope that she could one day meet his Jamaican family. She enjoyed his light hearted teasing and he was inordinately pleased if he could make her laugh. After a week or two of meeting for lunch, she had invited him to her house for dinner, where he had met her father and he and Calvin had liked each other instantly. After that, he was a frequent visitor to the house and her father would either disappear into his study or say he was going to walk down to the pub, leaving them plenty of time on their own.

When her father became ill, Martha was distraught and spent as much time as possible with him at the hospital. Calvin sometimes went with her and he could see how desperately ill her father was. He chose not to come with her every time, thinking to give them more precious time together; instead he would either telephone or call round to the house when he knew she had returned to see if she was all right.

Martha was grateful for his consideration but insisted her father wanted to see him. She was very glad of his support, his solid presence after each painful visit gave her a chance to let go of her emotions which she tried so hard to hold back when she was at her father's bedside. It wasn't until some time later that Martha realised how much she had grown to depend on Calvin and how much she was taking his comforting presence for granted.

After putting away most of the papers, Martha called Calvin and arranged to meet him after work the next day at a coffee house in the town. She had thought about just asking him to come to the house to tell him her news but had decided she didn't want to show him all the papers at once and so meeting him on neutral ground would mean she could feel her way with the story. This would avoid putting him under any pressure that he had to come with her, because she was determined to go to France and already she was tempted to ask him. She needed more time to think and anyway, she thought, they had never been away together before. She was determined that she would go with or without him and at that time, she didn't know if it would be possible for him to get the time off from work. Nor did she want to move their relationship forward simply because she was now living on her own. In her heart this was what she did actually want along with half the village, but it was too soon for her to make any sort of commitment. She enjoyed her job, her friends and her autonomy, nurtured by circumstances since the death of her mother. She needed the status quo to remain unchanged for a little longer.

Martha had taken some compassionate leave from her position at the Building Society and had also been told she could have more time off if it was needed to sort out her father's affairs. She still had some holiday time owing as well and this would prove very useful for her planned excursion to France. But for the moment she just wanted to share her new found discovery with a friend and Calvin was just that, a very good and kind friend.

The next day, she tidied up the house and then put the assorted certificates and documents into appropriate folders, with a whole stack ready to give to the solicitor, another to keep and a third, all the relevant information about Marilor and Abigail. In the evening, she decided to walk the short distance to the coffee house but decided she would not take any of the papers with her. The early September sun was still pleasantly warm on her skin and she was happy to see the blue sky, but still not quite able to lift her mood to greet its friendly caress. Calvin was waiting for her inside and had found them a window seat and had already ordered coffee. He looked at her questioningly; he could see she was not her usual relaxed and confident self. After a quick hug and a kiss he asked her,

'What's wrong? Has something happened?'

She started her tale cautiously, telling him about photos she had found and the amount of bills her father had kept. Then she told him about the letters and what they revealed, about the story of an unknown French woman called Marilor whom he had married and the tragic consequences because she had then seemingly turned traitor. How, years later, she had died in prison, possibly leaving a little girl who would now have no known parents, because her father was named on the birth certificate.

Calvin was stunned just as she had been, that her father had kept this first marriage a secret from her all that time. But apart from her father, these were people Calvin felt nothing for and so he asked her questions she might not have asked herself.

'How sure can you be that your father was the father of Abigail, might she have been the child of the German Officer? '

'Yes, that's possible I suppose, but the birth certificate does say her name's Abigail Ballard.'

'How old would she be now?'

'Well, she was born in May 1941 and this is 1980 so she will be thirty nine years old, if she's still alive.'

'Unless she died tragically or when she was born, there's no real reason why she wouldn't still be alive, if you didn't find a death certificate.'

Calvin then asked her if she had been able to read the postmark of the letter from Monsieur Rombouts. She told him that she hadn't thought to look for it and then she told him of her intention to go to France and find some answers.

'Great idea!' Calvin said, already excited at the prospect of an adventure which he was assuming would include him. His kindly approach to this whole discovery made her feel safe and protected and she started to feel that there wasn't a better person she could think of to accompany her and that going on her own actually held very little appeal.

And so they agreed. Martha phoned the Building Society the next day and arranged three weeks leave from work, one of which would be unpaid. Calvin also had no difficulty in arranging some time off as he was still owed four weeks holiday. They met early the next day to go into Maidstone on a shopping trip for a crawl in tent, a groundsheet and sleeping bags. Calvin had been to see his parents to let them know where they would be for the next two or three weeks and then after stuffing a few clothes and toiletries into the panniers they set off to Dover on Calvin's Triumph Bonneville, taking a chance on catching a ferry to Calais without pre-booking.

Their plan was to find Claude Rombouts, the Frenchman who had written to her father in 1955 telling him of the death of Marilor. All they had to go on was the smudged and faded postmark, the only visible words being St Pierre which they guessed would be a place in Northern France. As a youth, her father had lived in the south of England and the easiest access point would have been the northern coast and then on to a farming area. According to the maps they had bought and consulted while sitting on the ferry boat, there were several St. Pierres which included town squares and churches. But there was only one place which looked likely to have been from where Monsieur Rombouts had written his letter and that was Saint-Pierre-Sur-Dives, a farming town near Caen and so they made that their destination.

Once they were off the ferry and on their way, Martha had plenty of time to think about their hoped for meeting with Monsieur Rombouts. She loved riding pillion and enjoyed speeding through the towns and countryside on the powerful Bonneville, her fingers curled around the rear seat bar, the warm air on her hands and face. The first dying leaves danced and swirled in the wake of the bike as she soaked up the sense of freedom and the smell of the farms and flowers they passed. Now that they were in France, she was beginning to enjoy a sense of adventure which she knew she would not have felt had she embarked on this journey alone. They stopped a few times to stretch their legs and Calvin studied the map again and then they continued by following the road signs to Saint-Pierre-Sur-Dives. Soon after that, they came to the signs for *Centre Ville* where they parked in the pretty ancient town to look for a bar serving a *'menu du jour.'*

The owner of the cafe where they stopped, chattered to them in a friendly manner about where they had come from and then about the weather being so pleasant for September. Despite the sunshine, she told them there was a shortage of tourists for the time of year. Martha and Calvin did not understand every single word she said but were not going to feel faint-hearted about their lack of totally fluent French. After smiling encouragingly for her to continue, Martha asked,

'Connaissez vous Monsieur Rombouts? Je pense qu'il habite prés d'ici.'

'Oui, Mademoiselle, je lui connais, le Bureau du monsieur est en face du supermarché.'

They finished their meal feeling pleased and not a little surprised with the success of their progress so far. The cider they had with their meal helped ease the nervousness Martha was suddenly experiencing as she smoothed her chestnut brown hair and did the same to Calvin with a quick kiss on his cheek. They walked across the road to the opaque glass window with the name M. Rombouts on the adjoining door. Finding no bell, Calvin tapped on the door with his knuckles. It was opened quite quickly by a young woman who greeted them coolly and with some evident surprise as if she was expecting someone else. Martha took the lead asking if they could speak to Monsieur Rombouts.

'Avez-vous un rendezvous?' The woman asked and Martha had to admit that they did not. She felt like a

naughty school girl who had barged in to the headmistress's office without knocking.

'You must telephone first.' The woman replied in English.

Deciding she would not be put off by being bullied, she said.

'Please could you do that for us? We don't have access to a telephone.' The woman sighed and told them to come in and wait making it very clear from her expression that this was not the usual way of conducting business.

'I will check his diary,' she said and strode off, every line of her body indicating her disapproval of their intrusion and that she had more important matters to deal with. After five minutes she returned.

'Demain,' she said. *'Dix heure trente.'*

Martha and Calvin thanked her politely while being ushered out with a sweeping movement of her arm and a brusque, *'au revoir,'* but they were delighted with this achievement. They spent the rest of the afternoon riding around the town and the neighbouring farmlands and checking out possible places to camp for the night. This they found in a municipal campsite which had wonderful facilities for showering and barbecuing and cost what seemed to them to be very few francs. They bought baguettes and cheese and a bottle of wine, an opener and plastic glasses and played cards on a picnic table in the compound until the sun went down. They spent the next ten minutes giggling at the struggle they had to put up the tent in semi darkness, and then couldn't believe the smallness of the space inside the tent when it was completed. They cuddled and whispered together before finally falling asleep wrapped around each other.

CHAPTER 3

In the morning Martha and Calvin showered together, sharing shower gel and shampoo and making love soapily, feeling uninhibitedly sexy in the half empty campsite. Still damp from sharing the one inadequate towel between the two of them, they packed everything back onto the bike while eating the rest of yesterday's baguette. They rode back into the town and were ready and waiting at the door when Monsieur Rombouts arrived just after 10.30.

He was small built and dark haired in his thirties and they realised at once that this could not be the same man who had written to Martha's father. The Monsieur Rombouts who had written the letter would probably be at least into his sixties. Introducing himself, he greeted them charmingly, in English and apologised for his lateness, indicating chairs for them to sit on while taking papers from his briefcase. They were pleased to find that he was very courteous and did not display any of the tetchy characteristics of his secretary.

'So, how can I help you?' Suddenly Martha was a t a loss to know how to begin. Sensing her confusion Calvin stepped in.

'My friend's father has recently died.' Indicating Martha, he continued in his halting French.

'She found a letter that he had received in 1955 from a Monsieur Rombouts. Concerning the death of a woman called Marilor Ballard.' He finished awkwardly. Leaning forward and ready now to join in the conversation Martha said,

'We were expecting someone older, possibly your father?'

'Aahhh! 1955, yes, that would have been my father. He also was a *notaire,* a solicitor that is, like me. I took over the business from him several years ago but he has retired now. So is this a matter of inheritance? I believe you have come a long way haven't you? You are English?'

Haltingly they confirmed that they had come from England, but that it was not about money. In a mixture of French and English they told him some of the sad story revealed in the letters and certificates that Martha had found and then waited while the solicitor sat in thoughtful silence, apparently considering what he would say next. She finished by adding,

'We understand she had a child so what we really wanted to know is, Monsieur, does anyone know what happened to the daughter, Abigail?' Monsieur Rombouts shook his head continuing to look thoughtful and then finally said,

'An interesting story, I can understand your wish to know more but I'm afraid I don't know the answers to any of these questions. It's all a long way before my time. I think I must call my father; he has a good memory and may recall your father and possibly this woman as well. I'm sure he'll be able to help you.'

He dialed the number and waited. Greeting his father affectionately he then explained who his visitors were and why they were there. Very soon the conversation became rapid and more serious and Calvin and Martha were unable to follow the one-sided dialogue. It was evident that Monsieur Rombouts had no difficulty in remembering the French woman Marilor and how she had turned traitor and died in prison twenty five years ago. The conversation went on and on until finally the younger Monsieur Rombouts smiled at the now quite tense young couple in front of him.

'My father would like to meet you. If you would like, you will be welcome at his home later this afternoon. I'll give you the address and some directions, will that be all right?'

Chapter 4

Calvin and Martha were very happy with this kind invitation and set off to find the house of Monsieur Rombouts. It was an enjoyable ride away from the town and they took their time, not wishing to arrive too soon. Martha wondered if these country lanes and wide open fields of waving golden crops would have been a familiar sight to her father in those days before the war when he had worked on a farm and fallen in love with a young French girl. Her stomach tightened at the thought of her father's betrayal by this young woman, but then surely it was not entirely one-sided, her sense of justice reasoned, since he also had abandoned her with a baby. She tried to put any judgements out of her mind until they might hear the truth, as they pulled up outside the farm door. They were dismounting just as it opened and the slim elderly figure of Monsieur Rombouts greeted them.

'Entrez et bienvenue' he said, sweeping an expressive arm outwards and they followed him into a large kitchen with a solid looking wooden table big enough to seat at least ten people and covered by a patterned oilcloth. The room was dark from lack of windows after the afternoon sunshine, but still welcoming with its clutter of books and newspapers, cooking utensils stacked or hung, wire covered cupboard doors housing kilner jars and bottles, all apparently filled with home produce. Of Madame Rombouts there was no sign but her presence was strongly felt with this evidence of home cooked preserves. A saucepan of coffee was steaming faintly on the wood fired stove and was carefully served to them at the table by Monsieur Rombouts into three-tulip shaped mugs without handles, followed by a jug of warm milk and a dish of sugar lumps. A plate of tempting looking *petit fours* was also placed in front of them before Monsieur Rombouts finally sat down to join them with a satisfied smile. After a few polite exchanges he asked a questions about Martha's father in his charmingly accented English. She told him of her father's illness and subsequent death from cancer, how she and her father had lived together in the house near Maidstone following her mother's earlier death in 1965. She spoke in English and there were very few words that Monsieur Rombouts had any difficulty with but in any case, he had placed a large French/English dictionary on the table in readiness for their visit.

'I remember your father well,' he began. 'He was a polite and friendly young man with an appetite for adventure I think, because he came to our country with just a few clothes and a bicycle. He could not have been much older than fourteen years old when I first saw him. He told us that his father had died some few years before and that now he had left school he was at a loss for a career. He said he had an appetite for travelling before choosing and settling down with a career. His mother, evidently a liberal minded lady, was enjoying a new relationship with a man she had met at her work in the library in the town where I believe they lived. Jeremiah asked my wife and me for work in this small holding that we still have here today. Of course, I told him no, this is my hobby young man. I don't need any help! You could ask my neighbour Monsieur Piske, I told him, he has a large farm, many cows, even more pigs and all the land that is needed to feed them. And so that is what your father did. He obtained work from my neighbour and learned to plough the fields, use the milking machine and to clean out the piggery. He seemed to like the life on a farm and enjoy the work and of course he was also learning the language. Monsieur Piske had no wife that I ever knew, but he had two daughters, Janine and Marilor.'

Monsieur Rombouts was clearly happy to have some company and fresh young faces to talk to. An obviously personable and sociable man he continued chattily.

'Whenever your father Jeremiah had any time to himself, he would take Marilor, who was I think a year or two older than him, into the town on his bicycle, perched on the crossbar (here we had to check the dictionary) and no-one thought it was dangerous. They would play *boules* with their friends or whatever else young single people did then. You will know my friends that as time went on, those days were troubled with rumours of war but of course the young people only wanted to think about the present. By 1938, to them, war was still something disagreeable for old men to worry about. Sadly, time overtook us all as you know.'

Monsieur Rombouts spoke of these people as if they were very much younger than he was, but he could only have been a few years older himself. They all took a contemplative sip of coffee as the seriousness and sadness of those days seeped into the air like a grey mist. Monsieur Rombouts visibly collected his small frame together in order to continue his tale.

'Jeremiah did not want to go back to England at that time. Whether this was because he did not truly believe there would be a war or thought that, if it came, it would soon be over and would therefore not affect him. I don't know. He would have been about sixteen or seventeen by then and had growing feelings of *amour* for Marilor, the daughter of my neighbour Monsieur Piske. Who knows?' Monsieur Rombouts said this with a heavy shrug of his shoulders as if to say, who will ever understand the young? He continued.

'We will never know huh? But when the war came, it jumped on us country people with frightening speed. For many years we had lived with the undercurrents of unrest that came from Germany, like ripples from a stone tossed into the water, ever since that First Terrible War. I will tell you. Firstly there was the Treaty of Versailles, which Hitler took upon himself to ignore by re-introducing military conscription into his country. Then also, in 1938 he had taken a province of Austria, admittedly without violence, but it was not his to take.'

He said this with indignation, and then continued.

'He had a well-known hatred of Jews and was fanatical about the purity of the German race with a disregard for human life which was totally unparalleled and which he actively demonstrated in his love and belief in Eugenics. This was a programme adopted by a certain Doctor

Mengelés and paid for by the government, to experiment on or eliminate all people of supposed lower intelligence. He found his victims in orphanages and prisons and those he experimented on were never given anaesthetics.' Once again, the outrage in the little Frenchman's voice was tangible.

'Many died as a result or were permanently damaged or were unable to have children as a result. They promised male prisoners a shortened sentence if they would undergo a procedure to prevent them from having children. These men accepted, eager to accept early release from prison and not really believing in the consequences of an operation but also knowing that refusal would be punished. People were not nearly aware enough of the potential for evil that Hitler had.'

Martha and Calvin listened attentively to this brief history lesson, their attention caught and held by his obvious passion for the subject. Not wishing to interrupt and bring him back to the subject they had come to talk to him about, they resorted to the odd encouraging nod for him to continue.

'When Hitler invaded Poland at a town called Mora in 1939, Europe finally started to take notice. They realised at last the power of this man and so France and your own country, England gave him an ultimatum: to withdraw or War would be declared. He refused. It was September of 1939 and that was when our world changed. By 1940 Hitler and his Armies were everywhere. Japan and China were attacking each other, parts of Belgium had already submitted to Hitler. The northern parts of our beautiful French countryside were occupied all the way from Calais to Amiens. The noise of airplanes and bombing was dreadful. You cannot believe. The United Kingdom was bombed night after night. Guernsey was captured and then the rest of the Channel Islands. The Germans were everywhere and still there were countries who steadfastly remained neutral, but not Italy. No, Mussolini finally showed his true colours and took the side of this horrible man. Now we were seeing Germans in our streets, arrogantly driving around in their cars and wearing their shiny boots. Taking our food and our women.'

Mesmerised now by the old man's voice and the story he was unfolding, Martha ate another *petit fours*, almost without registering its sweet simplicity. But she couldn't forget they had a purpose in coming here.

'But what of my father?' she said, gazing at him.

Monsieur Rombouts folded his hands in his lap and appeared to come back from a distant place in his mind.

'Aahh, yes, young Jeremiah. Now, with the war spreading like a disease, he was not so happy and free from care. There were soldiers billeted all around the farm of Monsieur Piske and young Marilor, always a fun loving girl, flirted with the young German soldiers. And this was a dangerous thing to do. Even though some of them were quite polite, if you were wise, you didn't get too close.'

He paused as if deciding what to tell them next, and then asked,

'You know that we are not far from the river Dives? Our town stands upon this river. Unfortunately it is not a very well-behaved river, it meanders to and fro and then it ends up in a sand bank called the Cap de Cabourg, about one kilometre before La Manche, or what you call the English Channel. But let me first return to the story of your father, because he had fallen in love with Marilor and his youthful emotions had overcome his better sense. That summer was pleasant and during haymaking the two of them had enjoyed a wonderful time, making hay while the sun shines, isn't that what the English say? Marilor found that she was pregnant and whether this was true or not, she told Jeremiah that her father had insisted they get married. At the time, I think Jeremiah was happy with this and the marriage took place at the office of the *Mairie,* quite quickly and quietly. He hoped that she would settle down with a baby and stop flirting. Like many young men, he thought marriage and a baby would tie her to his side. But as time went on, Marilor continued with her flirting and Jeremiah was most unhappy. But there, the Catholic knot was now securely tied.'

'As I have said, Jeremiah was a hard working and pleasant young man. A helpful person. When British airmen found themselves falling to the earth from their airplanes, it was good for them if they could get to a farm undetected and find shelter. It was even better if they heard about an Englishman, not very far away, who they could speak to in their own language. They found that Jeremiah was willing to help them; he was youthful and adventurous and had the language to be able to liaise with the Resistance movement. *Voila,* his reputation spread. He felt honour-bound, a duty in his eyes, you understand to help these Englishmen and also the Canadian airmen to get back to England, especially as he himself was not yet old enough to join the fight. He and some of his friends from the village between them, they would see to it that many of these men who might otherwise have been captured were in fact taking a boat trip down the river Dives under cover of night to Cap Cabourg. This is a point near to the sea but it is not easily passable as I have said. There were others who would meet the boat and help them on the final parts of their journey back to British Quarters.

Jeremiah made this trip many times, I believe, bringing the boat back sometimes in daylight when the trip had taken too long due to the weather, or other unexpected hold-ups. It was very dangerous and we did not know all about it at the time of course. Certainly Monsieur Piske did not know and Jeremiah thought that Marilor also did not know. Now that they were married and living together at the farm, it must have been more difficult to arrange these nocturnal trips, but from what I heard, Marilor was not interested in what Jeremiah was doing, she was busy befriending the German Officers and staying out late into the night. You have to believe that she wasn't really a bad girl; she was young and pretty, misguided and also pregnant during a war when people were so unsettled and thought that anything might happen. The German Officers used people like Marilor to flatter and charm and bribe in the hopes that they would let some innocent piece of information fall which they could exploit. Perhaps Marilor now felt that she had tied herself up too young with marriage and a baby due to arrive in the winter. In her eyes Jeremiah had been exciting, foreign and new when he first came on to the scene, but now he was familiar to her and was quite ordinary and rather serious compared with these Germans. If they were all going to become German in the end, did it not make sense to get on with them, be on their side? This I think was her reasoning. We, that is my wife and I did not know very much about what was going on until afterwards. We certainly didn't know at the time that she was pregnant because it didn't show. I'm not even sure we knew she was married. I don't think Marilor fully understood the danger she was putting Jeremiah, her husband in, let alone herself, when she started to tell her German friends all those little bits of information. But it led to many things including aborted rescue trips which had been arranged by your father.'

At that moment, the spell was broken by the smiling presence of Madame Rombouts. She greeted them all with kisses to both cheeks as if they were old friends and then after exchanging pleasantries with her husband in French, she scolded him for neglecting their guests, despite the evidence of coffee and petit fours on the table. She brought out sweet white wine that she had made herself from elderflowers and small savoury pastries from one of the wire-fronted cupboards. She found glasses whilst shooing away several kittens with her foot which had followed her in. Time had to be taken for her to tell the names of the kittens, which all sounded very much the same to Martha, Minou, Minette, Mino and some others and their cuteness and habits had to be admired. They also had to be fed which Madame insisted was done outside in one of the barns, so the kittens were all tempted outside again and she left in a whirl of activity with dishes held high and kittens leaping up trying to reach them.

This sudden activity brought about a change in atmosphere which affected them all and for a while they sat in comfortable silence sipping the wine, wondering whether or not Madame was going to return and if Monsieur would resume his story telling. In the end after finishing their wine and pastries, Calvin took the initiative by politely suggesting they return the next day so as not to tire the old gentleman and using the excuse that they had to find a campsite for the night.

They stood ready to leave, gathering up their motor bike jackets just as Madame came back into the kitchen. She immediately vetoed their decision to leave and insisted they stay for supper and also for the night and would not hear any of their protests. She assumed they would sleep together and fussed around them finding blankets and handtowels, guiding them to a bedroom which she said used to belong to Mickel their son who they had met first in the town earlier that day.

Gratefully accepting and in fact not being given the chance to refuse they looked around the room. It had wallpaper of brown autumn leaves covering both walls and ceiling and a pink hanging lampshade to match a pink candlewick bedspread. They tested the bed for comfort, which was narrow, old and creaky. Accepting everything as being all great fun and probably a lot more comfortable than the hard groundsheet and sleeping bags which they had slept on the night before, they hung their jackets in the enormous cherry wood wardrobe and returned to the kitchen. The smell of *coq au vin* filled the room and was now bubbling away on the wood stove while Madame peeled potatoes at the sink. She beamed at them, instructing Monsieur to pour more wine while she told them how much they had liked young Jeremiah and how he would sometimes call in to see them for an aperitif before going off for his evening adventures, whatever they might be, usually a game of *boules* she thought.

Martha felt strangely comforted, surrounded by so much warmth and acceptance coming so suddenly into her life. Just a few days ago, she had felt bereft and confused. Now, with the solid, confidant presence of Calvin by her side and listening to the stories about the War and about her father as told by Monsieur Rombouts, she felt attached to these people by a strong bond. They were on her side, accepting her with their kindness and sympathy and they had known her father well, which pleased her. When she had first read the letters from France, sitting alone in her house in England, she had felt betrayed by her father, by his secrecy and by the revelations which might show he was not the man she knew. Now, having met these people who did not appear to be judging him, she felt a little better about the privacy with which he had surrounded his past life, understanding that perhaps it was he who had been betrayed and that he would have wanted to start afresh after the horrors of the War.

The four of them continued to sit in the kitchen, eating and drinking. Martha and Calvin listened to tales, not of the past now, but of their life since, with their family of children and grandchildren, of pets and farming. Tomorrow would be soon enough to continue the story and hopefully hear something about Abigail. Tonight she and Calvin would take comfort in each other in a country and in the company of a family she now knew had been close to her father.

Chapter 5

Martha awoke to the raucous sounds of a cockerel crowing and for a fraction of time she wondered where she was. Sounds from the kitchen drifted up to them and she felt the warmth of Calvin's body beside her and moved her leg across his to see if he was awake. Definitely awake, Calvin rolled over onto her, pinning her arms above her head and kissed her mouth, whispering conspiratorially.

'They're downstairs, make love to me!' He stroked her body and her back arched in response to his strong brown hands. Holding his head close to hers, they made love slowly and sensually taking and receiving such pleasure as neither of them had known before. Satisfied but both wanting more, they were afraid that someone might come and fetch them so they hurriedly washed in the bathroom next to their room; the smell of coffee was enticing and they were eager and ready to taste it.

Madame was fussing over the wood stove, her cheeks glowing from the warmth which was not really required on this mild September day, but it was apparently essential when cooking. She was wearing a fresh blue nylon overall with no sleeves and Monsieur was sitting at the table as if he had been there all night long. Coffee with milk was served in large bowls with croissants hot from the stove and placed in front of them as they exchanged morning greetings.

Martha licked her fingers not wanting to waste a single buttery flake. Monsieur watched her until she had finished then suggested they take a stroll outside to feed the chickens, admire the vegetable garden and generally take the air. By now he had lit a cigarette which was filling the kitchen with the strong smelling French tobacco he liked and his wife was shooing him out of the door waving her hands under her not inconsiderable nose. Calvin and Martha were happy to wander through the gardens and appreciate the views of rolling farmland, so peaceful now from when her father had lived near here and yet essentially unchanged. While walking, the old man continued his story.

'Jeremiah used to call in and see us on his way out in the evenings. He never confided about what he was doing or where he was going and we understood that the less we knew the better it was. As my wife said, he would take an aperitif with us, Calvados or Pastis, just a small one, you understand and he would hold it up to the light and say, 'Dutch Courage' and toss it back down his throat quickly. We didn't understand what this expression meant and he could never quite explain it to us.'

Martha tried to explain it as well, because as she also told him with suddenly brimming eyes,

'For the first time, you have told me something about my father that I can recognise. He used to keep a bottle of Pastis in the cupboard and he would occasionally pour himself a glass, mixing it with water. As a child, I used to like seeing it go all cloudy and then he would drink it all in one go and say 'Dutch Courage' just as you say. I never asked him why he said it, I just accepted it the way you do with your parents. Now I can see that he must have been remembering a time when he lived here.' She brushed a hand across her eyes and Calvin took it from her gently and kissed it in sympathy, a touchingly romantic gesture for him. They had come to a bench under some chestnut trees and Calvin suggested that it looked like a good place to sit. Then he asked,

'Was it very dangerous, what Jeremiah was doing?'

'Ah, yes, it was. He had a boat that was almost all handmade, a battered old thing he had rescued and patched. The river is not the best of rivers. Sometimes it is narrow, sometimes it is wide, some places it has a lot of weeds and debris. Of course he did not go all the way to the sea; it was too far to go in one night and the boat was not suitable. So this involved other people, other boats, other venues. It was risky. He didn't tell us what he was doing but my oldest son, Stefan, he used to talk about helping Jeremiah to mend his boat and such like. Of course he was just a small boy then and we warned him to stay away from the Germans. We didn't want him involved in anything; naturally, he was just a little boy and we wanted to protect him. He lives in Caen now with his family but he would remember your father, he knows the story now of what happened then. Most people who were old enough would have known afterwards what was going on and they would still remember it now. Jeremiah was kind to Stefan and would let him hang around him because during those years my wife was often ill. She had several miscarriages during the war, probably caused by the stress of it all and she wasn't always able to look after Stefan but she trusted Jeremiah to take care of him if she had to take to her bed. Michel was not born until 1945. That is why there are a lot of years between them, nearly nine years, because of all those miscarriages.'

'And so,' he continued, 'in those early years, while Jeremiah was off fixing his boat or helping his fellow countrymen, Marilor, who worked in the restaurant and bar in the town was meeting and flirting with the German Officers. She met them in the bar or sometimes we would see her being picked up by a car on the road into the town. The Germans gave her gifts of cigarettes and meat, which had probably started off its life on her own father's farm. They bought her drinks and they chatted to her in a friendly way and she enjoyed their attention. She seemed unaware that they were asking her questions which could get her husband into serious trouble. They didn't know she was married, she never wore a ring, or that she was pregnant because those were things she didn't tell anyone. The Germans would ask her, where is Jean-Claude or some such person, this evening? He's good fun, they would say and she would reply, he's down by the river with Jeremiah catching rabbits. Jeremiah, isn't he the English boy? That's him she would say. Just the fact that he was English was enough to catch and hold their interest. What was he doing here? Did he work? How old was he? More and more questions would follow and more and more information would have come out. Was she stupid? You may ask. Yes, she was a little, naive maybe but more than that she was greedy. For attention and for flattery and for material things.' Here Monsieur Rombouts' whole attitude changed his small frame stiffening with indignation or some inner fury; it was hard to tell what fired this little man's excitement.

'I did not like her father; he was a nasty man who was not kind to his animals or his daughters. At first, I felt sorry for the girls having such a father and no mother to guide them. But Marilor wanted flattery, she wanted their gifts and she did not believe the Germans would act on her words. But they started to make more demands about what she knew and one of the Officers in particular paid her very special attention. She became infatuated with him and that was when Jeremiah at last became suspicious. He had trusted her, not knowing just how friendly she had become with these men. She had become careless, blasé you might say, and then he suspected she might be having an affair with this one officer. One day, Jeremiah confronted her and they had a terrible argument. He asked her if he really was the father of her unborn child and she taunted him, hinting that he was not. She accused him of being more interested in the safety of his English friends, silly games as she called them, than in anything she did. She implied that she was revealing all his secret associations, dates and plans to her German friends. I don't know if she did this or even if what she was telling him was the truth. She may have had ambitions, I don't know, of being looked after by a rich German Officer. It was unlikely that Jeremiah was going to be rich if he stayed on the farm. Whether she was trying deliberately to upset him to bring things to a crisis point, I don't know, but in the face of possible exposure, Jeremiah panicked. He came to see us and told us some of what he had been doing and also what his silly wife had been saying. Up until that time we had never asked and he had never told us. He respected our wish to stay out of trouble because with my position as a *notaire*, we were respected in the community. But of course, we all knew certain things were going on. We tried to persuade Jeremiah that his wife was just immature, that she couldn't be the one who was making so much trouble for the English airmen. But he was adamant and in truth, we were worried for his safety. He told us he was going to leave that night using the same routes with which he had helped the airmen. He said he would stay in touch and he gave me the address of his mother which would be where he would be living in England. But he never wrote, and that is the address to which I wrote years later with the news of his wife's death and how you found me, my friends.

Chapter 6

His story told, Monsieur Rombouts folded his hands in his lap and looked at them both enquiringly, his white eyebrows raised. Martha, in an unconscious reflection of the old man's movements, lifted her own hands high and let them fall heavily into her lap. This was not the end of the story for her and feeling frustrated, she didn't know what to say. Her mind was still absorbing all this new information and yet there was still so much she didn't know. She thought she had known her father, who he was, but of course there is always a life a parent has before children come along. They had been so close, just the two of them for so many years. Now she had discovered that he had not one, but two marriages which had ended tragically in death. Jeremiah, the young man, sounded passionate, adventurous, a risk taker and she tried to link this to the responsible citizen, the reliable, comfortable man she had known, a man who liked Pastis but had never shown any interest in going to France. She had always assumed he had spent time there during the War, just because he had joined the air force on his 18th birthday. But that would have been after his return from this quiet farming community near Caen where they now sat enjoying the sunshine. She knew he could speak French and she had also assumed that he had learnt the language whilst serving his country. Now she knew that it was already familiar to him. There were still so many questions burning her lips.

'So what happened to Marilor after my father left?' she asked. But Monsieur Rombouts was tired and was reluctant to continue.

'Later my dear, first I think we will go and find some coffee.'

Martha stood up quickly, immediately feeling remorseful at the amount of time they were taking up as well as all the generously proffered meals they were eating. Trying hard to follow his mood, she suggested they all have lunch in the town, their treat she said, but Monsieur was adamant that this would not suit his wife. Calvin then offered to take his motor bike into town and buy some provisions but this was also met with a frown of dissension. Calvin was restless and keen to be a little more active, so he suggested to them both that he and Marilor could ride into town to buy one of those delicious looking fruit tarts from the *boulangerie*. This was met with the approval of both Monsieur and Martha and so they left the old man to have another cigarette while they sped off into the town.

They bought a flan, beautifully decorated with peaches, strawberries and pears, as well as some flowers for Madame Rombouts and some fruit to eat later. Then while they were there, they searched around to find the bar where Marilor might have worked all those years ago. There were several; the town had a beautiful ancient covered market place and attracted many visitors from time to time keeping all the bars busy and today was evidently market day. They turned the bike to the road which led back to the farm, the closest to the route Marilor might have taken on her walk to her home. They found a possible contender, but now it was nearly lunch time and the café was filling up with people coming from work to eat and drink. Never the less, Calvin went to the bar and asked for cigarettes and while waiting for his change, he asked the barman if he knew the Piske family. The man looked at him strangely. No, he was told, they moved away years ago. Calvin sensed the unspoken hostility and hoped it was against the family and not him personally. He didn't follow up with any further questions and they continued back to the farm.

When they arrived, Madame was ready with an early lunch. This was quite a formal affair compared with their usual hastily snatched sandwich and an apple. Fresh bread and cider were placed on the table. The cider was chilled and still, not bubbly like they were used to in England. It was served in the same bowls they had used that morning for coffee and was smooth, golden and only faintly sweet, refreshing and delicious. Then they were served with a small salad sprinkled with a tangy dressing and fried *lardons*; this was followed by a pork stew which Madame called a *ragoût* and told them proudly that it was a traditional dish, popular in Normandy and cooked in cider. After this came a plate of cheese, *brie, camembert* and *fromage du chèvre* for them to help themselves and which they ate with a knife and fork on a plate of lettuce with a vinaigrette dressing. They unanimously agreed to save the fruit flan for later and settled for tiny cups of strong, sweet black coffee.

Both Monsieur and Madame Rombouts then took themselves off to the bedroom for an afternoon rest. The young couple, politely disguising their surprise decided to explore their surroundings for an hour or so hoping that Monsieur would continue his tale later on in the afternoon. Martha was looking thoughtful and so Calvin suggested they took the motor bike back into the town. He went up to their temporary bedroom to fetch their jackets and by the time he returned, Martha was looking close to tears.

'What's up?' he asked, perturbed at her sudden change of mood. Martha took the leather jacket he was holding out for her.

'I can't believe my Dad just upped and left her! She was his wife and she was pregnant, for God's sake! And we still haven't heard if she is alive or dead!'

'He was young, Mattie, a lot younger than we are now. His life was in danger, can you imagine how he must have been feeling? All the risks he had been taking to save those guys, which she suddenly put into danger, through some sort of vanity. He must have felt she didn't care about his life or theirs. She sounded like a real silly tart, literally, I'm afraid. I'm sorry but I'm with your Dad. And look, she even said it might not be his baby, didn't she? Perhaps he knew it wasn't his.' He held out her crash helmet and watched her with sympathy as she strapped it on. How could he not feel sorry for her? They had made a rapid start to this adventure but her emotions were still in chaos after the death of her father less than a month ago. The discovery of the letters and all that it had led to had followed so quickly. He thought about their own relationship as well, which had taken on a new dimension, sleeping together every night and being together all of every day. It was a lot of emotionally charged time and perhaps it was too much for her all at once. But he was loving it, he had to admit. This was the first time he had taken the bike abroad and after quite a few casual girlfriends, he was enjoying these new feelings of closeness and intimacy with Martha. He was interested in all the stories about the war as well as Martha's search to find out about this part of her father's life which he had kept so well hidden. He understood why she was feeling tender and was determined to help her to keep it all in perspective. It was not in the least surprising she was feeling vulnerable he thought, giving her a hug.

'Come on, let's go and find the river.' he said and she smiled.

'You're right, I know. It just feels so strange. Now I don't know whether I've got a half sister or not, do I! OK, let's find us a river. We might have more luck with that.'

Calvin kicked the bike into life and they roared off once again towards Saint-Pierre-Sur-Dives. They parked in the centre of the town, fixing their helmets to the handle bars. It was still warm so they carried their jackets with them. The market was busy in the beautiful ancient medieval building, lively with colour and movement and the murmur of voices. They moved through the aisles with difficulty as men and women stopped to kiss and chat with no thoughts of holding anyone up. Their purpose there today was more to do with meeting and greeting than buying. Martha lingered over the little brown rabbits in cages, which Calvin cynically told her, 'They're for the pot.'

They saw tiny yellow chicks and ducklings as well as full grown chicken bought for egg laying and which were pushed into boxes then tied with string ready to take home by their new owners. Outside in the street, there were clothes, skirts and jumpers including the inevitable array of nylon tabards like the one Madame Rombouts had worn that morning. Row upon row of shoes, gloves and belts; tables laden with cheese, eggs, bread, fish, meat and vegetables. There were so many things to eat that they wondered how the supermarkets did any trade at all. Some of the market traders just had a small table selling a few garlic bulbs and onions or leeks, all home-grown. Others had large and prosperous stalls and were selling produce from much further afield.

Martha and Calvin relaxed into this typically French atmosphere, buying cold meats and cheese from a stall not yet packed up and baguettes from the Boulangerie to take back to the farm. They bought a flagon of Calvados in a pretty pottery jar as a gift for their hosts. They asked a young man to direct them to the river and he pointed them towards a crossroad in the centre of the town and told them which road to take. They decided it would be just as easy to walk but first they packed their purchases all into one bag and returned with them to the bike. They packed the bag into the panniers and set off again on foot.

Their route took them past bars, shops and even an old cinema. They took the turning the young Frenchman had indicated and found the Auberge and Chambre d'hotes he had told them to look out for. The river ran next to the road and at one point it went underneath the road and then meandered on through the garden of the Auberge. They looked at the river's steep sides and saw how high the water might have come in winter. Was that another reason, she wondered, why her father had left when he did? Perhaps the river was too high in wet weather to conceal a boat with its illicit stowaways and its stealthy passage through the night. But in fine weather, there would have been places to hide here, the road bridge was probably once a conventional raised wooden bridge and would easily have concealed a small boat. There were trees further along, poplars with great round clumps of mistletoe attached to them, sprawling willow trees in untidy masses and quite a few oak trees, which from their size would undoubtedly have been growing there 40 years ago. Talking and wondering if this was where the daring rescues could have been carried out, Calvin pointed out that these same trees would have provided good cover in the darkness. But there was no-one around who they could ask; even the Auberge looked closed and they concluded that it probably opened only for evening meals and overnight visitors.

It was time to return to the farm. The town was swiftly emptying, streets were being swept and tables and umbrellas folded. The market was over for another week, although the larger stalls would surely be going to another venue the next day. Ten minutes later they were back on the bike and heading for the farm, having agreed they really couldn't continue to take advantage of the hospitality so constantly offered to them by the Rombouts and they should find a campsite for the night.

CHAPTER 7

Inevitably, the Rombouts did not agree with the young couple's decision to leave. When they arrived they discovered that the younger son Michel whom they had first met in the town was visiting his parents. He had naturally been updated with the story since the day they had met and he had been intrigued. He added his voice to his parent's, insisting that they stay at least another night and that it was very pleasant for his parents to have friends to stay, it was good for them, he said. Martha was only slightly reluctant in agreeing to stay, she was still anxious to hear about Abigail.

They sat around the table in the now familiar kitchen; Madame had removed her nylon tabard and replaced it with a loose cardigan, her concession to changing for dinner. Once again, she was the only person in the room with things to do; fussing over the kittens and then shooing them out, putting more wood on the stove;

placing glasses and an opened bottle of sweet white wine on the table along with a bottle of Pastis, a small jug of water which had its' pouring lip unusually placed at right angles to the handle instead of opposite. The fruit tart Calvin and Martha had bought earlier was now cut into small manageable slices and yet another meal of bubbling meat was filling the kitchen with its' herby aroma.

They each took a piece of tart followed by a glass of wine, silently savouring the fruity flavours. Then Michel sat back relaxing into his chair with his half empty glass saying,

'I spoke to my brother today and he remembers your father quite well, considering how young he was at the time. He was only about four years old when your father left for England but apparently he was always ready to play with him. Stefan said he used to follow him around quite a bit. He said he would watch your father mending his boat, hammering bits on, sticking bits in. He remembers where all this took place as well. He, your father that is, would take Stefan on the crossbar of his bicycle to where the river goes under the road near the old Auberge. He would drag the boat from under the bridge up onto the bank and set young Stefan up with a fishing rod to keep him quiet no doubt, while he did things with the boat.'

'We went there,' Martha said, 'today! We thought it was a possibility, didn't we Cal?' Calvin smiled his agreement, pleased to see Martha was back in a happier mood.

'So, did you know Marilor?' she asked Michel tentatively, almost afraid to hear the answer.

'No,' Monsieur Rombouts senior answered for him 'By the time Michel was born, Marilor had gone.'

'Where did she go?'

'First of all, she went away, to have the baby. Not many people knew about the pregnancy because she left the farm to live with her sister for a while, for her confinement. Her sister was married by then and lived in Falaises. Marilor had kept her pregnancy a secret from everyone and so it was not evident if you see what I mean. Then in 1942 she returned with her sister, her brother in law Hervé and their two children. At least, everybody thought they were both Janine's children. The little girl was called Abigail, just a little baby but we knew from what Jeremiah had told us that this may have been his child. Janine and her husband had come back with her children to help the father, Monsieur Piske, because he was finding it difficult to run the farm on his own. The house was big enough for all of them to live in quite comfortably and now that Monsieur Piske no longer had the help of your father, he had found it very hard to manage on his own. So now the problem was solved again, for all of them.'

Monsieur Rombouts filled the kitchen with smoke from his newly lit Gauloise cigarette and without any further prompting he continued.

'Marilor had not changed. In fact I think she had hardened, she was acting very pleased with herself, maybe because she had got away with something. She played with both the children like any aunty would but left all the care of both children to her sister. Nobody would have known that Abigail was Marilor's child and in fact I often wondered whether even her own father knew, despite the fact she told Jeremiah he had insisted on a marriage because of the pregnancy. She never mentioned Jeremiah and of course, he had left to go back to England by then. She didn't wear a ring and she was completely free from care. So, she continued with her evening work at the bar and also with her friendships with the German soldiers. She would listen to the conversations of the French lads and she would re-tell what she heard to the Germans. If she heard about an airman being sheltered in a barn somewhere, the Germans would hear about too. Of course, we didn't know about any of her treachery at the time. We didn't know it was her.'

'The Wehrmacht were occupying the North of France at that time, right here where we live. They were camped not far away and we felt their presence every day. Sometimes, we even felt sorry for them, so far from home and most of them were quite polite when they spoke to us, but if they wanted your chicken, a pig from the sty or the fruit from your orchards, you couldn't say no. You handed it over and went hungry yourself and became poorer every day. Saying no was not in the language of Marilor either and I think her treachery was suspected by some. There was a family who lived not far from here and they were all particularly nervous around the Germans. We suspected the wife was probably Jewish. All Jews were requested by law to go to the police station and state that they were Jewish but this lady did not go. She didn't want to be separated from her husband and was in any case only half Jewish or possibly even less than half. But one night she was arrested and sent on a train to Drancy, which is near to Paris and where, we later discovered many Jews were sent for internment and then later still, to be sent onwards to Auschwitz. Her husband was devastated. Nor did we know of their fate in that horrific place until after the war was nearly over. It was terrible.'

Monsieur Rombouts' small figure drooped with the weight of depression that these memories were stirring in him. His son Michel put a consoling hand on his shoulder.

'Enough I think, it is time to eat and take a rest from this sad talk. Maman, I will help you to serve the dinner and we will forget about those dreadful days for a while.'

And so another evening passed of less anguished talk, eating deliciously tasty food followed by a game of cards their hosts called *'Belote'* and which Michel tried to teach them. Similar to whist, it was more complicated for the young couple, who resorted to pieces of paper to remind them of the newly learned values of the cards. They lost track of who was winning as the wine went down and the laughter increased. The evening light turned purple over the fields which hid so many past secrets of untold pain. Acts of valour as well as acts of deceit and treachery were all now safely covered by wheat and maize and grazing cows. Madame Rombouts declared herself ready for bed and Michel said *au revoir* to them all and returned to his apartment in the town. Martha and Calvin said their 'Good nights' and left Monsieur with his cigarette smoking contemplatively by the stove, a kitten curled on his lap. Taking off her clothes and folding them, Martha said,

'Well we know now that Abigail lived for at least a year! It's great to be hearing all this other stuff about my father and the War and all that, but when are we going to hear what has happened to Abigail?'

'I guess he'll get round to it in time. He probably doesn't realise its significance to you, perhaps. Maybe tomorrow we can push him a bit.'

Chapter 8

The next morning, Calvin and Martha decided they really must be strong and make a break. However, they were again pressed into staying another night. It was as if Monsieur Rombouts was re-living the past through his story, which he had not done since the war and was reluctant to let them go. At the same time, he also appeared to be reluctant to speak about Abigail. So they decided they would go out for the day and leave the Rombouts to recover from the extra work they were creating by staying there and from the effects that the traumatic tale was having on the old man's spirits in particular. Martha felt the need to distance herself from their story teller at least for a while and to reflect on what they had learned. Maybe that evening they could steer the conversation the way they wanted it to go with more resolution. So having made their excuses but agreeing to return that evening, they set off for Caen.

The road was clear and very pleasant to ride through, the rolling country side easy to see for miles around, green and gold against a blue sky with a few wind combed clouds. They had by-passed the town on their approach from the north of France but now realised that Caen was a very big place. Having heard so much about the War, they thought they would look out for a Second World War Cemetery and found one quite quickly at Banneville la Compagne, a memorial burial ground for French soldiers. Each tombstone had a small bed of planted flowers in front of it and they were aligned in square soldierly rows, which somehow captured the essence of the young obedient soldiers whose lives they represented. Both of them found it immensely moving and studied the lists looking for familiar names but could find none that they had recently learned. There were 2030 identified graves and representation of a further 130 unidentified soldiers, statistics which they knew were just a drop in the ocean of the final figures. After stopping to eat their baguette and cold meat from the day before, they decided to carry on to Bayeux where there was another cemetery, this one was for British soldiers. It was a much larger cemetery and the gravestones this time were all in the forms of white stone crosses, dazzlingly bright in the sunshine which these brave men would never see. Martha was grateful for the turn of fate which had sent her father home again and not left here in this foreign land, despite the many risks he had taken. To see these orderly rows, each one representing a mother's son, so many lives taken, was heart-breaking. How thankful she was that his life had been spared.

In sombre mood they returned to the now familiar route through St Pierre-Sur-Dives and the farmhouse of Monsieur and Madame Rombouts. After such an emotionally laden day, it was fitting that they return to the subject of Marilor and her weak and wicked ways. Martha was impatient to hear what happened next and in particular, what happened to Abigail.

Madame and Monsieur Rombouts had eaten their last meal of the day and so they all settled down for the evening waiting for the old man to start again on his story. But hearing where they had been, he was once again lost in his memories of the War.

'For several of the War years, life continued in its usual pattern, at least for us, although we knew that terrible things were happening throughout the world. After the shocking attack on Pearl Harbour in Hawaii, where so many thousands were killed or wounded at the American airbase, so many ships and submarines sunk or damaged, we thought nothing worse could happen but of course, it continued. But this was the kind of news that was beginning to affect your father. He was almost eighteen and felt compelled to return and join in these efforts to destroy the evil which was sweeping across the world.'

'The Japanese were intent on slaughter and destruction and their decision when asked to withdraw, was not to surrender. You might say that this was their religion, their culture. The result was that the Americans took that most wicked reprisal on Japan when they dropped an atomic bomb on Hiroshima, destroying lives and crops which left its mark on the land and on the health of the people for years afterwards. The Japanese continued in their resistance to surrender, because of their fanatical belief in death in preference to withdrawal and a further terrible act of reprisal was inflicted when another bomb was dropped, this time on Nagasaki.'

Monsieur Rombouts carefully lit another cigarette before continuing reflectively.

'But of course, a year before all that was the D Day invasion in June 1944. This was the most incredible co-ordinated assault on the beaches here in Normandy involving land, sea and airborne troops amounting to thousands of men. It had taken months to prepare and yet it remained a secret from the Germans, the only information leaks were deliberate ones to mislead Hitler into believing that the attack would be on Calais. So the impact was superb and was a turning point in the War.' Here the old man chuckled with the memory, but continued immediately.

'By 1945, Russia was acting independently and had captured Warsaw in Poland. The only good thing about it was that those dreadful camps were discovered at Auschwitz, where so many of the Jews had ended up. So much wickedness was revealed. Hitler had camps in Germany for many years before the war as I mentioned earlier, where he allowed experiments to take place on gypsies, dwarfs, prisoners, even twins and many other people who had unusual or different bodies. People whom he considered were inferior beings, people of low intellect, criminals or just orphans and now those numbers included Jews. Doctor Mengalés was the devil behind these experiments and their aim was to breed an Aryan race. And now the full horror of his Eugenics programme was coming into the light because as I said before, they used these poor innocents for experimentation, without anaesthetics before discarding them like ants. Many of them were killed under the knife; others were executed or sent to one of these camps.' Monsieur Rombouts stopped to collect a bottle of Calvados and some glass cups, taking his time to pour them all a cup of coffee from the stove and top it up with the Calvados.

'Yes, our lives life continued quietly in contrast to those atrocities. Marilor continued to go to the café every evening and often brought home some little treats of food. The family accepted these without too many questions. The War was drawing to a close. All the while, Englishmen were found and imprisoned as were Jews, though not many of those. Janine was suspicious. She had a suspicious nature you understand, probably because she was not nearly so pretty as her sister. She did not like the looks that were exchanged between her husband and Marilor. She often accused them individually of flirting. She would also ask Marilor in her sharp voice after one of these sudden arrests of people accused of harbouring either a Jewish person or a potential prisoner of war,

'Did you know about this? What do you know?' She accused her of being too friendly with the Germans, too friendly with everyone. Old man Piske was impatient and irritable with all of them. And then another bad thing happened. It became apparent that Marilor was again pregnant and this time she did not have a husband to hide behind. Janine questioned her, 'Who is the father?' We don't know what the true answer to that question was, but Marilor told her that it was the German, the one she liked especially. She was in a very difficult position to tell the truth, because if it was Hervé, Janine would have killed her or possibly him too, but if it was the German soldier, she would not have been much better placed. She was as they say, between a rock and a hard place and either answer was doomed to get her into trouble. She did not think her sister would tell, but there was jealousy and animosity between the two sisters. It seemed to Janine that Marilor got away with too much.' Monsieur Rombouts lit another cigarette, looking at his wife and then sitting back in his chair, a far away expression in his eyes. He looked strained and they again realised the toll this story was taking on him.

'It was the end of the war and arrests were being made by then and everyone was accusing everyone else. Janine had no compunction about pointing the finger at her sister. She preferred the neighbours to believe in Marilor's treachery than that her own husband might have fathered the unborn baby. Marilor was led through the village with other collaborators to the Germans, chained to each other by shackles around their wrists and their heads shaven. They were a terrible, terrible sight. Some were crying, others were shouting defiantly back at the crowds who taunted them. Shame is a powerful tool and Marilor was crying now. They were all taken to a prison near Bayeux and many were executed. I don't know why, but Marilor was saved. She lost the baby whilst she was there and maybe because of this, she had some sympathy. There were not many who were prepared to speak against her in a legal way; her sister, yes, but few others. Some say she was in the hospital when the executions took place and she escaped the death warrant simply through a clerical error. I don't know what to believe because by then, she had few admirers and fewer friends.'

Monsieur appeared to have pulled himself together as he carried on in a more business like tone. Martha looked across at Calvin and showed him her fingers were crossed and he nodded, a tiny movement of his head.

'I wrote to your father about her death because the prison wrote to me as her solicitor at the Notaire's Office where Michel is now. I never knew whether he received the letter, he didn't acknowledge me and I wrote it in a formal way and not as a friend. Somehow, I felt those days were too far behind us and we had never kept in touch, despite our promises.'

'Janine was bitter and she quarrelled constantly with Hervé, her husband. She still did not know if he had been unfaithful to her with Marilor and he knew that she probably never would find out. He denied it always as any Frenchman would. She never visited her sister in prison as far as I know. Nothing was going well for her, her father, old man Piske was dying and so there was much more work to do. I'm not sure what his illness was, but he stayed in bed all day, the doctor sometimes calling to give him extra painkillers because he was evidently in a great deal of pain. I don't know any of the details. Hervé was running the farm with Janine but their life was overshadowed constantly by the past and she was a very unhappy woman. She had grown to hate the child of Marilor, Abigail, and in a fit of bad humour, she took the child to the Abbey and abandoned her to the nuns, telling them she could not afford to feed this extra mouth. No-one dared to criticise her decision and if they questioned her, she told them the truth, that Abigail was not her daughter and therefore, not her responsibility. It was a hard line to take and the family was already ostracised and believe me, it got worse after that. The child that was left behind, Jean-Paul, used to cry all day, Stefan told me. When the old man finally died, they sold the farm and moved away. I have no idea where they went and I think that was how they wanted it to be. They disappeared into total anonymity as far as I knew. And that, *mes amis* is all I can tell you.'

'So Abigail could be still alive?' said Martha.

'Yes, she could.' The old man said. 'She was alive when her mother died in 1955. After that, I don't know.' They thanked the old man for all he had to tell them and he waved their thanks aside with a nicotine stained hand.

It felt to Martha as if they had both been on a long and arduous journey, one which was emotionally draining and because Calvin had been there beside her all the time, he was also now a part of her life. Just one week ago she knew nothing of Marilor and now she found herself judging this woman who had so disrupted and altered the lives of so many other people, including that of her own father. An unborn child had lost its life in a prison; another child was who knew where? Questions, questions and still she didn't know where Abigail was.

That night, Calvin and Martha made love tenderly and lovingly and she drifted into sleep once again wrapped in his arms. Her dreams were fragmented as she moved restlessly. White foaming waves crashed around her, intent on dragging her under and faces loomed out of their green depths pointing at her. Briefly, she saw her father, fit and well and young as she had only ever seen him in photographs. He was surrounded by tiny round boats each one containing a baby who pointed and cried. She awoke suddenly as all the babies started to reach out to grab her. Now wide awake and shivering in the early morning light, she pulled on her jacket over her T-shirt and slipped on her leather boots and softly crept down the stairs, out into the still, sharp air. She could hear the rustle of the cows in a neighbouring barn as she stood and watched the sky infusing with pinks and oranges. She felt there was something missing, an uncomfortable subconscious knowledge that she was unable to identify, that maybe the dream knew something that she didn't and was trying to tell her. Filling her lungs with the fresh clean air she tried consciously to relax and to feel more at peace with herself. Smiling at the perfidy of her dream, she went back inside to see if Calvin was awake.

Chapter 9

They ate a leisurely breakfast and then left their hosts amidst a flurry of kissing and handshakes and a last look at Madame Rombouts incredibly tidy *potager*, with its neat rows of lettuce, beetroots and leeks. They said their goodbyes to the miniature goats, (two females and four kids born that year) and the kittens, one of which Martha pretended to tuck inside her leather motor bike jacket. They exchanged addresses and promises to write and to come back before their final return to England. They also had the addresses and telephone numbers of Michel and Stefan which Monsieur Rombouts had insisted they might need or find useful.

Martha's house in England was very different from this lovely old stone farmhouse with its orange tiled roof and large, comfortable rooms. By comparison her house was small, or at least all the rooms were small although there were more of them. It also stood very close to the neighbouring houses which were almost identical except for a few changes her father had made over the years. She wondered if her father had made those some comparisons when he had first come to live in this region all those years ago. It was those years that were now occupying her mind as they sped through the lanes, the rhythmic thudding of the engine vibrating through her knees and relaxing her.

With all that she had learned, she knew now that her father's knowledge of France and all things French had originated from his time spent here as a youth. At the age of 18 in 1941 when he had returned from the north of France he had joined the Royal Air Force, not as a pilot, romantic though that would have been, but as a passenger in an aeroplane sent out to reconnoitre the land. He was there to take notes, make sketches and to take photographs and keep the home base up to date on success of missions and any other noteworthy goings-on or unusual sightings. She realised he had probably never been back to France since leaving in 1941. He stayed in the RAF for several years after the War had ended and she now felt able to confirm her guess that the letter from Monsieur Rombouts telling him of his wife's death had probably instigated several major decisions in his life at that time. Another turning point to equal that which he had made at the age of eighteen, another path chosen. One of his decisions would have been to leave the RAF after 15 years of service and another was to marry her mother, buy the house that she now lived in and then to settle down and start a family.

Martha felt the bike slowing down. Lost in her own thoughts and without having taken very much notice of where they were going, she saw that they had arrived at a seaside town.

'Moules et frites?' Calvin said with a smile as he propped up the bike, took off his helmet and then shook out his black hair.

'Good idea,' she said. It wasn't difficult to find a restaurant and they sat outside with an enormous pot of steaming mussels with their glistening blue black shells all open to reveal succulent orange and white meat and smelling deliciously of garlic and wine. They alternately dunked chips or fresh white bread in the sauce and laughed at the mess they were both making. Afterwards, they strolled on the beach eating mirabelles (small, sweet yellow plums that Madame Rombouts had insisted they take with them) and resolved to treat themselves later to a night in a *Chambres d'hotes* where they might also be able to have a bath, wash their hair and maybe even wash some of their clothes. The narrow French bed at the farmhouse had given them a cautious taste for comfort. Despite its creaking lumpiness, it had proved to be warmer and more comfortable than a ground sheet. Tomorrow they would go back into Caen and find a library or some such place which could offer them information about a prison that had once housed collaborators or perhaps where they could find the Abbey where Abigail had been left all those years ago. They spent the rest of the day alternately walking the beaches or sitting sipping coffee in the bar/tabacs along the way until they found a *Chambre d'hôte* which had rooms to let.

The next morning they again set a course for Caen. The lovemaking of the night before, some cleanly washed clothes and bodies and the leisurely pace of a day on the beach had worked its magic. They had washed away some of the depression brought on by so much of Monsieur's morose storytelling and now they were in the mood for sightseeing. Their attention was easily caught by Caen Castle, former residence of the Duke of Normandy and looking far too interesting a place to ignore standing as it did, right on their route into the town. It had been built by William the Conqueror as a place to prepare for the ambush on King Harold and whose battles were so famously re-told in the embroidered tapestry at Bayeux. The huge fortressed enclosure was insufficient to entirely protect the building inside against the bombing which it sustained in 1944 and now the walls housed a history museum displaying many works of art.

Strolling around the chambers showing the artworks on display, they were stopped by some friendly Americans on holiday and who, on hearing their English voices, were delighted to be able to speak in their own language and share their experiences. They told Martha and Calvin all about their pilgrimage to France which was a mission to discover where members of their own family were buried having come to the aid of the War in France.

'Forever young,' the woman sighed, 'so incredibly sad.' The couple had visited the Normandy beaches where so many battles had taken place; they had also been to the War Museum and the American Cemetery in St James and which they said was about two hours further south. High up on the hills away from the town, they had found this peaceful cemetery very moving, particularly those graves bearing a star, indicating soldiers with Jewish origins. The woman confided that they too had Jewish origins and were thankful that the War had ended when it did. They had found family names amongst the thousands of graves which they said had made their journey worthwhile. The next place they wanted to visit was St. Mère Eglise, the famous church where an American paratrooper called

John Steel had hung suspended by his parachute from the church spire while German soldiers chatted beneath him leaving him stranded but undetected for many hours. The town had been occupied since June of 1940 and it was on the night of June 5th 1944 during the Normandy D Day landings that the airman found himself so precariously dangling over the enemy. He was eventually sighted and cut down by the Germans who arrested and imprisoned him only to be later released by the Americans when they liberated the town in the following days. The pair listened fascinated to the story which they were told proudly had been immortalised in the 1962 film, 'The Longest Day.'

Martha then told them a little about her own mission. The friendly Americans helpfully directed them to the regional council offices and Town Hall, telling her that it was a good place to make enquiries and which they had passed earlier. They said that it looked very much like an Abbey which instantly caught Martha's attention. Thanking them for this useful exchange, they said goodbye and were wished good luck in finding lots more which would help Martha on her quest.

'Isn't it amazing?' Calvin said. 'All those years have gone by and yet we can't get away from it can we? I never realised. The War is still all here, all around is.' They continued on foot to find the Rue Guillaume le Conquerant and the location of the Town Hall and maybe the Abbey as well.

Chapter 10

As they walked, Martha talked to Calvin about her parents. Her father had always been a quiet man she told him and she knew that he and her mother had been happily married, albeit it had lasted for only ten years before the premature death of her mother. She remembered her clearly as petite and with dark hair, straight and shiny as a chestnut like her own. But mostly she remembered the fun they had together and her kindness. Thinking back, she realised her mother must have been well known for her generosity of spirit, because there were always other people's children in the house, sometimes by invitation to tea as company for Martha but at other times, she knew that her mother was often asked to look after somebody's child as a favour, because they were not always the same age as she was. Thinking about it now, she wondered if her mother had wanted more children, she was sure she had enjoyed their company and would not have taken money for looking after them. Her mother made everyone welcome, baking biscuits and greeting everyone with a happy smile. By comparison with her gentle father, her mum was the cheerful, outgoing energetic one. She had missed her dreadfully when she died and that early period of her life was shrouded like a cloak, blurring many of the more unpleasant details of her death and the days and weeks of sorrow which followed that even now, she couldn't recall without pain.

Aged only thirty five, her mother had died of a brain haemorrhage, an accident waiting to happen, her father had told her in explanation of the swiftness of her illness: a blood vessel in her head with a weak wall which had burst after several days of suffering a severe headache, it could have happened at any moment in her life. The suddenness of it had shocked them all, especially her grandmother on her mother's side who looked as if she had aged overnight, becoming old and unwell herself. The funeral was seared into Martha's memory as a time of silence, it was such a contrast to her frequently noisy mother and in her memory, that veil of silence continued for many months until she finally got used to the quiet and empty space with a child's stoical acceptance.

Her father had not outwardly changed with the death of his wife although Martha and he had grown closer, her mother's joyful personality notably missing and lost to them both forever. He tried to compensate for their loss by taking her out more often, little trips to the sea, to animal and bird sanctuaries and to the cinema but she missed the company of the children that her mother had always encouraged her to play with. Sometimes she went to friends' houses but the logistics of this seemed to be too much for either her father or her grandmother to cope with. They both preferred everything to be as organised and unchanging as possible while he was at work. So the pattern had been for her grandmother to pick her up from school until her father came home from work and also to look after her in the holidays. Her grandfather had died a long time ago and her grandmother had a man friend whom Martha liked. He was old, of course, but he tried his best to make her laugh with jokes and tricks, but mostly he would find programmes on the television which they could both watch. Thinking about him now, Martha remembered that it was Pops as she called him, who had told her several things about her father that she hadn't known before, such as his having served in the RAF in the War with a job that involved taking photographs and drawing maps. 'He must know Germany like the back of his hand,' he would say. France too, thought Martha to herself as she and Calvin walked down the long road to the Abbey.

The Town Hall was indeed a magnificent building, built onto the southern transept of the Abbaye aux Hommes, a huge Romanesque Abbey built by William the Conqueror in 1067. William had been responsible for founding this Abbey and his wife Mathilda had founded a sister abbey, the Abbaye aux Dames as penance to the Catholic Church for being married to each other as they were first cousins.

They went into the very grand *Hotel de Ville* or Town Hall hoping to find out if the Abbaye aux Dames which they had just discovered existed was the place where Abigail had been left. They were directed to the mayor's secretary, who although appearing helpful, was perplexed by their questions and not able to help them very much.

However she did suggest they look in a telephone directory for Abigail's name and also told them that The Abbaye aux Dames was open to the public now and that up until four years earlier in 1976 it had been used as a charitable extension to the social network, looking after orphaned and disabled children. This was better news than they were expecting. They were given the address of the Abbaye aux Dames, which was back towards they way they had just come, in a road called Place de Reine-Mathilde. They were beginning to feel tired now after all their walking.

The telephone directory was not very helpful, because it was listed firstly in villages or towns and where Abigail lived was something they had yet to find out. But looking at the phone book gave Calvin an idea. Why didn't they phone Stefan? He didn't live far, just the other side of Caen and Monsieur Rombouts said he had known her father. Maybe he had also known Marilor in the brief time during the war that she had remained on the farm.

They found a place to sit down, rest their feet and have a sandwich and make a plan. After they had eaten they would first find the Abbaye aux Dames and then see if they could contact Stefan. Everyday felt as if those past years were getting closer.

Chapter 11

Jeremiah sat in his boat, crouched and cold under the half moon of light dappling between the trees and sparkling on the ripples on the river. A sleek brown rat glided silently close to the water's edge, its eyes round and bright and ever alert. He heard the rustle and crunch of a cautious footfall and waited. An owl called and he answered the sound with a similar one of his own and Hugo slipped down beside him. He looked at the pale thin face of his friend and saw that he had serious news to impart. Their greeting was a swift clasp of hands and Jeremiah waited patiently for Hugo to regain his asthmatic breath. After a few moments he was ready.

'August Mennen is at the bar with Marilor, I heard them talking.'

'Is it true then? What did they say?'

'They were seated away from everyone, it was difficult but I stayed behind the door of the urinals and could hear your wife. She is a bad one, that one. She was asking him, pleading with him to take her back to Germany. She said her father was abusing her, molesting her and she must get away.'

'That's nonsense! He is not a very nice man, I know, but abuse? Abusing her? When, may I ask?'

'Calm yourself, my friend, you will be heard! I agree, she just wants to have an exciting life I think! It's probably not true. But that's not all.' Hugo stopped to regain his breath again, his hollow chest heaving with the effort.

'She told him about you. She said you were the one that got messages through and met the Englishmen. So be very wary Jeremiah, they will set a trap for you. I heard that Hans Mennen had a cousin down river and the whole story is confusing. He is not like the others and I don't know what his game is. He is German, he is using your wife and you must abandon these rescues. You will be caught and shot and so shall I. Take your boat and go.' Jeremiah was scared. These were very deep waters now and if the Germans knew then his life was about to end quite soon if he stayed.

'What about Marilor?'

'Do you still love her, after what she says about you?'

Jeremiah was miserable, he couldn't think straight. How had his life become so complicated so quickly? What a rash fool he had been. 'If I ever get out of this mess, I will never speak to her again. Does that answer your question?'

'She's pregnant isn't she?'

'Yes Hugo, she is pregnant but not with my child. I just want to get away from all this now. I've had such good times on the farm and in the bar with you and the others, I see now it has to end. Tonight, I'll take the boat down the river and take my chances. You have been an excellent friend, the best. Goodbye Hugo, I shall drink to your health in England.' The two friends embraced and Hugo once again slipped away through the trees. Jeremiah thoughtfully tied the boat under the bridge and then with a heavy heart, he sought out his wife at the Bar.

Marilor saw him coming through the door and clung more tightly to her German soldier. Jeremiah's face coloured with fury but he ignored her and instead he asked for a Pastis at the Bar. With his drink in his hand and refusing the offer of water to mix with it, he walked over to the two of them. He sat down and coolly appraised them both for several uncomfortable seconds. Marilor looked at her soldier but he avoided her eyes and held Jeremiah's stare. Then, tossing back the strong liquid in one swift movement, Jeremiah slammed the empty glass down on the table and left without a word. Much later that night, he made his last trip down the River Dives.

Jeremiah knew he would miss France and his thoughts were angry and confused. He had packed a little fruit and some bread and also stowed his bicycle in the boat. Messages which would normally have been passed through his friends to help a rescue this time had been left unsaid. He had enjoyed his few years with the farming community, had learned some very colloquial French from the laconic mono syllabic farmers and his accent was authentic, having never been tainted by an English tutor. But he was by no means bi-lingual and his papers were not French, in fact he didn't have any papers, not even the recently introduced English temporary passport. He had pulled on a dark jumper and beret and hoped to be taken as a young French boy, at least by the Germans, should he be stopped. When dawn reached through the trees and the waters beneath him glistened less richly in the moonlight, he thought he would abandon the boat and continue by bicycle. He knew the rendezvous points and would hide and wait until a sailing boat could deposit him safely on the shores of England.

Chapter 12

Stefan Rombouts was a farmer, unlike his father and brother. He had a reasonable sized farm on the north east side of Caen with a herd of about forty cows. He rented some neighbouring fields, enough to grow the food to feed his dairy herd and a little extra to sell on if the crops had been productive. His memories of life during the war were fragmented and mostly unhappy. His early memories of Jeremiah were of sunny days and pleasant trips out with each of them teaching the other new words which made them both laugh. But that had changed after the sudden disappearance of Jeremiah which he had not understood at the time because no-one had explained it to him. Thinking back on it now, Stefan knew that the memories which followed that time had been sustained for him by his parents whereas his own memories were the ones which he knew in his heart were more genuine, even though they were emotional rather than factual. He remembered his father as being a self righteous man who kept himself aloof from the neighbours and was involved in legal matters which occupied his mind to the exclusion of all else. His mother he remembered was constantly ill which he now knew was due to the many miscarriages she suffered and which understandably also caused her great sadness and depression. But the affect on him was to feel a paucity of love.

By the end of the war, his brother Michel was born and although his mother's illness and depression lifted, she turned all her attention to the new baby and he received even less attention than before. He used to play with his cousins and also the two children belonging to Janine, a little boy called Jean-Paul who was the same age as he was and then much later, the little girl called Abigail. Hervé, their father was often asked to take the children into town to get some shopping, because he was one of the few people who had a car and could drive and Stefan would sometimes go along with them too. But here his memory was confused, because Abigail wasn't always with them although they still saw her because they were visiting her at the Abbaye aux Dames where she now lived. Jean-Paul and Stefan were told very clearly by Hervé that they must not tell anyone about these visits and this felt like a large burden for the two boys, one which in Stefan's case, fuelled an increasing anger and bitterness against the world. He felt sorry for Abigail, who he thought might feel just as lost and neglected as he did and he would ask the nuns if he could stay with her. His parents only had eyes for his new baby brother and were unaware of his resentment.

He grew up in the shadow of his younger, cleverer and more handsome brother and determined to move away as soon as he was able, to follow his desire to become a farmer. He left school aged fifteen and went to work on a farm close to where he now lived. He stayed friends with Jean-Paul who had since moved away and one of the ways in which they would meet was at the Abbaye where they both went to visit Abigail, who was then aged ten. He and Jean-Paul would take a walk by the river and eat the fruit they had brought with them then get back on their bicycles to go to the Abbaye. They were both fond of Abigail and the nuns were pleased she had some contact with the outside world. She told them something of her life in the Abbaye and to the teen-aged boys it sounded very boring. Their own lives were quite hard, both working on a farm as they did, but Abigail had gardening chores as well as housework to do all of which were arduous and seemed to take up all of her time. The orphans had to do everything from making their own beds to the older ones doing the food preparation and cleaning in the kitchens. There were a lot of children and the nuns took the responsibility for their education as well as giving them a home. Visitors were rare as most of the children did not have any family although a few did, but poverty or illness kept them away. So the children were isolated from the village and with all their chores there was very little spare time for enjoyment or leisure pursuits.

Because of their duties and perhaps because the Nuns did not see the value of integrating the children into a normal life, visiting times were restricted but also conversely, supervision for visitors was scant. So when Stefan and Jean-Paul were there they took full advantage of this lack of supervision to take a look around. The place was vast and it was easy to creep about in hiding, which Jean-Paul in particular was fond of doing. He had begun to look forward to these exploits, more than his alleged reason for being there, namely to visit his sister. Because of this, both boys had their first sexual experiences at the Abbaye but for Jean-Paul, this was not one he wished to dwell on. He hadn't liked it. His grandfather, old man Piske and also his mother were always scoffing at his weakness and squeamishness and now he had discovered that he found the whole sex act with girls anathema to him. He started to hate girls and the first target for this hatred was Abigail.

He was sixteen years old when Abigail asked him, not for the first time, why her parents never came to see her, because by then, even Hervé no longer came. On this one occasion, Jean-Paul was resentful and fearful and in the face of her questioning he became wildly angry and shouting at her, he said,

'Don't you understand you stupid cow, they're not your parents, they're mine. Why else would you be here?' She was horrified, having always harboured the belief and hope that one day they would come back for her. But she knew in a heart dropping moment that he was speaking the truth because as he had said, why else would she still be here?

After that and despite his angry response, she questioned him frequently on who her parents were, but he was off-hand and could only tell her that her mother was his mother's sister making them cousins and that she must be dead and he didn't know who her father was. After that, Jean-Paul made no pretence that he was coming to visit so that he could see her, because his motives were much more devious. Primarily, he just wanted to go wherever Stefan went. Then after this, his second motive was to gain sexual pleasures with the girls at the home, to see if his first experience was unique. He found out that it wasn't, he hated the girls, their femininity apparent in puberty and their differentness in general and so his interest then turned to the boys. Following up on his instinctive fascination with Stefan, he suggested that they tried some experiments but Stefan was disgusted with him and their relationship very soon deteriorated after that. Jean-Paul continued with his search for gratification and went to all sorts of lengths to persuade the young boys at the orphanage to come with him, to show him mushrooms growing under a bush or whatever he could think of at the time that would entice them into a hiding place where he would either cajole or bully the young boys into submitting to his will. To touch, to investigate, to probe. The boys became wary and afraid of him and this excited Jean-Paul all the more. At last he had found a sexual act which thrilled him. He didn't have to threaten the boys not to tell, that was the very last thing they would do.

Stefan was not interested in the exploits of Jean-Paul but it made him realise how easy it would be to do the same with the girls. Young and sexually awakened he didn't think about the consequences this might produce. One of the older girls Marie-Louise, a nervous and shy girl normally but who had fallen for Stefan's moody and dark good looks, had been coaxed by him into the bushes where he had seduced her. As a result, she became pregnant. She was terrified and told him he must do something about it. Stefan was also terrified knowing that he could not support a child or a wife and the reprisals would be too frightening to contemplate, so he did nothing. After that he stopped going to the Orphanage at all and so it was Jean-Paul who told him the terrible cost of his actions. Marie-Louise had been found in the toilets grotesquely hanging from a beam. Worse still, she had been found by Abigail and the sight of that discoloured, swollen tongue and distended eyes had made her sick. She then had to tell the nuns and they questioned her endlessly on what she knew of Marie-Louise's state of mind and why she would have taken her own life. It was a terrible sin and worse still that it had happened whilst she was in their care. Abigail swore she knew nothing and the pregnancy, still in its early days was never discovered. But she told Jean-Paul that she did not want him or Stefan to visit anymore, particularly, as she pointed out to him coldly, he was not her brother and he didn't actually come to see her anyway.

Stefan was shocked and mortified. For the first time in his life he was faced with a situation for which he was directly responsible, although he tried very hard to justify it in his own mind. She was willing, he told himself and she had snatched at those moments of exhilaration into her miserable life. He thought perhaps they were both guilty but she must have been mad to do such a dreadful thing as to kill herself and in such a terrible way.

He became obsessed with work and with his desire to have a farm of his own one day. His father had spent money on educating Michel; he would approach him with his own ambitions and see if he would do the same for him. Meanwhile, he worked for anyone who would pay him and slowly built up a smallholding in the farm on which he worked. He bought bullocks and sold them on and started to build up a stock. When he was able to tell his father of his success, he was genuinely pleased at the result it produced because his father gave him enough money to rent his first field with cowsheds and a shack in which to live. He was growing up at last and guilt and compassion drove him back to visiting Abigail at the Orphanage.

Chapter 13

Martha and Calvin had been unable to find a telephone box in order to warn Stefan of their proposed visit so they had continued on their way to his house. It had been surprisingly easy to find the right road with their detailed map and then to study the board at the start of the road where it showed the name of the house where Stefan lived. Hopefully he would be half expecting to see them they reasoned; his father would surely have telephoned him before now.

The roar of the Triumph had signalled several dogs to start barking and the noise in turn had alerted Stefan. A short, broad shouldered figure in overalls and gumboots emerged from a barn to one side of the house. Assuming this was Stefan, Calvin walked towards him with his hand outstretched saying in his best French,

'Hello, I'm Calvin Bradshaw and this is my girlfriend Martha Ballard. I hope we aren't intruding, did your father mention we might be calling in?' Stefan put down the bucket he was holding and responded with what could only be called a grunt although he did shake the proffered hand.

'I'm really sorry if this is putting you out, we just thought we'd say hello.'

Stefan picked up his bucket again and said, not as ungraciously as it sounded, *'Allons-y.'* (Let's go.)

Stefan shrugged of his boots and overalls by the door and sat down, indicating that they should do the same. The kitchen was large but it lacked the warmth and comfort that was so immediately evident in his parents' house. The difference was palpable: there was no sign of anything in this room which did not have an essential purpose. Calling it minimal, Martha thought to herself, was being kind and made it sound fashionable. This was stark. She gathered her confidence to ask if she could use the toilet and Stefan indicated the barn outside. Once there, she found a door in the corner of the cluttered barn and was glad to find that it had a proper pan and not a tray set in the floor. There was a hand basin and also a galvanised tin tub hanging on the wall which she realised with something approaching horror, was what the family must use as a bath. Sure enough, there was also a hose lying on the bare ground which led to a tap from a small water heater in the main barn. Enough to put anyone off having a bath in the winter she thought to herself.

Re-entering the kitchen she found that coffee was now simmering in a saucepan on the ancient looking gas stove and Calvin was doing his best to explain to Stefan where they had been and how they had found the Abbaye aux Dames. Did Stefan remember Martha's father? He was asking. Looking a little more relaxed and willing to talk,

Stefan replied, speaking slowly for their benefit but still in French.

'I was only four when he left, but such was the talk around him at that time that I still remember him, probably because he was nice to me and my parents always had other things to occupy themselves with. Yes, I used to go with him to the river and he taught me about fishing. When I have the time that's still my favourite pastime. I don't go back to the Dives very often, these days I go to the River Orne in Caen.'

'Do you remember Abigail?' Martha asked anxiously.

'Oh yes, I know Abigail. She went to the Orphanage as you say and I used to visit her there. Actually that's where I met my wife. Abigail stayed at the Abbaye until she was fourteen as an orphan. By that age she knew a bit more about her background. My school friend Jean-Paul was the one who told her she was not a Piske and that the Englishman Jeremiah was her father. Jean-Paul stopped coming to see her after that or at least, when he did come he didn't bother to talk to her. His main objective was to meet other girls and the boys who were there; Jean-Paul had problems of his own, sorting out his head, because he is homosexual. I didn't have much time for him, he was always too intense for me. At that time you know, it was illegal and he could have been put in a mental institution if anyone had found out. Of course now, in the 1980's it's all different and I believe he lives openly with another man. I've lost touch with him although he probably still goes fishing. Abigail and fishing were the only things we really had in common, that and the fact we grew up for a while in the same village and are the same age.' With a dismissive and very French shrug Stefan continued.

'I stopped going to see Abigail about that time as well. There was a girl at the home who killed herself and Abigail blamed me. I suppose she was right, indirectly as I may have got the girl pregnant. I was very young and I didn't know how to handle it. It's not something I'm proud of, but naturally I didn't expect the poor girl to take her own life. She hung herself and it must have been terrible for Abigail because she was the one who found her.'

Stefan poured himself coffee then held the pan up in a question for confirmation that they both also wanted more.

'Anyway, about two years later, my father told us that he had received a letter from the prison where Abigail's mother, Marilor was held and that she had died, I think it was from pneumonia compounded with malnutrition. After hearing this I felt bad about not having been to see Abigail. This was the first time I had heard the full story of her real mother being a traitor and being in prison. I was a bit older by then, more mature I suppose you could say and I felt sorry for her and bad about the way we had fooled about and taken advantage of the other girls there. Up until then, I had accepted that the Piske family were just too poor to look after Abigail. In his usual way, my father did not want any involvement with this news of her mother's death and was assuming Abigail would have been told about it, either by the prison or by the nuns. He had no intention of seeing her or doing anything more about it. I was very angry with him for being so unsympathetic. I believe the only action he took was to write and tell your father and so, as no-one else seemed to care, I went to see her. It was I who had to tell her and of course she was very upset in her way but I think she had lived for years with the knowledge that no-one was bothered about her. That changes a person you know. She said she was shocked to know the truth but that it made sense to her. She didn't cry. She said she had never understood how Janine could have just abandoned her at the home and then never ever visited her. I think she took some comfort from knowing that in fact her real mother had been given no choice in the matter. I believe Hervé still occasionally visited her but I'm not sure about that.'

'This all happened when she was nearly fourteen and Abigail was worried about where she was to go. I was glad that I had started visiting her again, because she needed someone outside the home to talk to, I think that made me feel better too, that I was doing something useful. The Abbaye had looked after her for ten years but now they had a policy of finding foster homes for the younger children, especially the babies. It costs a lot of money to look after so many children and although the social services helped them financially, apparently they relied heavily on legacies and the generosity of supporters and donations and there were not many of those, not after the War. They wanted to find a job for Abigail, preferably one where she could live in. She was fortunately a pleasant and willing girl and by then she also often helped in the kitchen. One of the nuns suggested they train her in the kitchen as a cook, she already did chores there, so she worked there for the next two years. Now that she was almost independent, she was allowed more freedom although there were still a lot of extra duties as well as a fair amount of praying! I was just pleased she didn't decide to become a nun herself.'

'So that was how I met my wife, Nathalie. She also worked in the kitchen; she was older than Abigail and was the one who taught her. Nathalie works in the town now, in a restaurant called 'Le Chat Noir.' She was unable to have children, a source of sorrow for her. Well for both of us really, so we adopted two from the Orphanage, a brother and sister, Bertrand and Nicole. They are at school now but they will be home soon. My wife was happy to be able to do this, she sometimes says she is glad she couldn't have children or we would never have adopted.' He smiled, his slightly gruff exterior melting a little.

'Do you still see Abigail?' Martha asked softly, a little afraid of upsetting his mood.

'No, I'm sorry, I don't. Too busy and it was a while ago last time I saw her. Why don't you stay around and wait for my wife to come home? She keeps in touch with Abigail occasionally and she'll be back soon.' Shrugging as if to shake of the past, Stefan stood up. 'Right now I have to go and milk the cows.'

They all walked outside together and watched as Stefan went off with the dogs to round up the cows. There was no garden, just a square of grass bordered by a low fence and the only evidence of children was a football lying abandoned and waiting. Everything was swept and tidy in the front of the house and further over, there were several chestnut trees sprouting from misshapen trunks along the raised perimeters of the fields with a straggling display of pink and mauve wild flowers on the banks beneath them. These and the still green leaves of the trees were a small and colourful oasis in amongst the dark twisted shapes.

At that moment the school bus arrived at the bottom of the lane which led to the farmhouse and two children jumped off. They assumed these were Bertrand and Nicole, the two adopted children who looked about eight and ten years old and were heading straight up the path towards them. The children stopped to admire the Triumph motorcycle and this provided a good topic for

Calvin and Martha to catch up and begin chatting to them about. Both children were immediately accepting of the two English people they had come home to find and were then hauled in turn onto the seat by Calvin to see what it was like. They admired and rubbed and patted the bike before reluctantly leaving it, then each child dragged an adult by the hand to show them some puppies. These were tucked at the back of a barn which normally housed the bullocks when they had to be kept inside. Martha thought they were delightful, both the children and the puppies were so sweet and she found the enthusiasm of both puppies and children infectious. It was hard to keep up with their excited chatter in heavily accented French and Calvin finally resorted to mime, which they thought was very funny. They played with the puppies, evidently the result of a stray hound from the hunt, four brown and white balls of fluff with overlarge heads and unsteady legs, until their mother returned from work.

Nathalie had driven up to the farm in a shabby red *Deux Chevaux* car and on seeing the motorbike, had already gone in search of Stefan to find out who their visitors were. Anticipating her questions, he met her on the path and told her what he knew of Calvin and Martha. She was an unusually tall woman and rather gaunt looking with her hair cut short in a severe style and already sprinkled with grey, but she was smiling as she came hurrying over to the barn. She greeted them in friendly fashion and then asked them to stay for supper which, with the children bouncing up and down encouraging them to say yes, they accepted. This was to be a simple rabbit stew which she brought out of the car, obviously already cooked and brought from the Café where she worked She asked the children to lay the table while she heated the stew and prepared a bowl of salad to serve with bread and cheese. Water and cider were also put on the table but not wine.

Now that everyone was seated, the conversation once again turned to Abigail and her possible whereabouts. Nathalie agreed that she was still in touch with her but not very often. She occasionally phoned her from work and she agreed to phone her later and find out if Abigail would see them; she thought it best if she spoke to her first because as far as she knew, she pointed out, Abigail was unaware of the existence of Martha. She then went on to tell them more about the Orphanage and that all the children had been very closed about their personal circumstances, even if they knew them, which she doubted. They all had different backgrounds and talking about what had brought them there whether it was rejection or bereavement, was painful to most of them. Her own situation was typical she thought, because she had been found abandoned outside the doors of the Abbey when she was just a baby. She didn't know when her birthday was or anything at all about her parents. So, she told them, although they were all different from each other, they were all in the same position at the home and were respectful of each other's privacy. After some prompting from Martha, she told them a little of what life was like.

'It was OK; the nuns were neither kind nor unkind. The rule was that you did as you were told at all times. If you didn't, you had to do extra chores. They didn't physically punish us because the work was hard anyway and extra work was punishment enough. The Abbaye is huge as you know and some of the nuns were closeted away from us, so we never saw them because I don't think they were ever the same ones who looked after us. In any case, we looked after ourselves and each other for a lot of the time because almost every chore you can imagine was performed by the children. The nuns ran the schools and here, the pressure was not about achievements, just about obedience. Academically, we were never pushed or even encouraged, as long as we didn't talk in class and produced the work that we were set to do, you could stay out of trouble. We were never castigated for getting the work wrong, just for disobedience.'

'It sounds awful.' Calvin said. 'I suppose they saw rules and obedience as the best way to run the place.'

'That's right. But it wasn't so bad. It was fair and not malicious, it could have been worse. We saw the nuns as being from a different planet, or at least I did, I thought they were barely human at all. The way they dressed, their quiet voices, their constant references to God. They ran the home meticulously from the point of view of keeping our records and also teaching the children their lessons but very, very few of them showed any feelings towards the children. Some of the younger nuns obviously liked the babies. I sometimes think now, that everything they did was as a penance, but they would have us believe that it was for the love of God and of his children.'

'Hardly any of the children had visitors and so when anyone of us did, the others would always be quite curious and sometimes would gather round and stare. Visiting was just on Sunday afternoons unless it was a holy day and then we would have extra prayers instead, because of course we had prayers every day as well. One of the nuns would see the visitors in to the common room, or the garden if it was fine, but she wouldn't stay to supervise. This was the time when some of the children were taken advantage of by visitors and they may even have been abused. Sometimes I think this might have even been the main purpose of an adult's visit and the person from outside didn't necessarily know anyone at the home at all, they just had a name they could mention at the door and were told where to meet the child. Then two hours later a bell would sound to tell the visitors they had to leave.'

'The fact was, the Orphanage served a very necessary purpose for us children, and we were fed and clothed, educated and kept warm. We didn't complain because there was nothing wrong that we knew about and no-one to complain to. In many ways we were better off than if we had lived in a poor or abusive family outside. What we lacked was love from an adult and so we gave that to each other. The way the home was run ensured that the older ones looked after the younger ones and the newcomers and this nurtured the bonds between us. The saddest part was when someone died from illness or left to go to work, because this almost invariably meant losing touch. The nuns always tried to find work in a live-in situation, whether that was working on a farm or the military or child minding, something like that.'

'Did they find work for you and Abigail?' said Martha.

'I worked in the kitchen and then I left to marry Stefan, but yes, they found a job for Abigail after a year or two, in a hotel. They liked to move people on to provide vacancies for the next children reaching fourteen. She works in Paris now. When I phone her later I'll let you know tomorrow how I get on, before I go to work. We can't offer you a bed for the night,' she continued, 'but if you would like to set up your tent in the field you are more than welcome.'

Calvin and Martha accepted gratefully, especially as dusk was falling. They had enjoyed their supper and the children were now in bed. Stefan was leaving the cows out for the night as there was no threat of rain and so he had finished work for the evening. He took a torch and showed them where to pitch their tent before wishing them goodnight. He walked back to the farm still carrying the torch and left them alone to spread the groundsheet and put up the tent in the fast dwindling daylight. Martha found some night lights while Calvin unrolled the beds. They struggled into clean T-shirts for the night and huddled together under a nearly full moon which cast its cold glow on the shining eyes of the cows.

'It's my birthday tomorrow. I'll be twenty four." Martha said with a small shiver. 'It'll be really strange without my Dad.'

'Let's celebrate then. Let's go to Paris anyway, whatever Nathalie says after her phone call to Abigail.' They kissed goodnight and tried to get comfortable, having to get used to the hard ground all over again.

They were awoken next morning by the sound of cows lowing, apparently eager for milking to start. They heard the distant rumble of the school bus and quickly dressed, guessing that Nathalie would also be leaving for work very soon. They were right because minutes later she was by her car tooting the horn to attract their attention, not wishing to dirty her shoes walking across the field before setting off for work. Realising it must be later than he thought, Calvin hurried across the field to greet her as Nathalie started to speak.

'I phoned Abigail and she said she would meet you this afternoon, I hope that's OK? She's at the Campanile Hotel, Paris, here's the address and telephone number. She said 1500 hours and to ask for her at the Reception desk. She was very surprised I think but she is looking forward to meeting you later. I'm sorry but I must go now or I shall be late for work. I have to prepare meals ready for the lunch time in the café. There's coffee in the saucepan in the kitchen, you just need to heat it. Say good bye to Martha for me because I really must go now. Stefan will be in the milking shed if you want to say goodbye to him.' Handing him the slip of paper and giving him a quick wave she jumped into the little red car which sprayed a plume of dust behind her as she disappeared up the lane.

Martha and Calvin took their time over their coffee in the empty kitchen. They helped themselves to the rich full cream milk standing on the table. Studying the now very creased map spread on the table they reckoned it would take them at least three hours to get to Paris. If they left soon they could have lunch on the way as this would probably be easier than trying to find somewhere in the City. So after tidying up the kitchen they went back to the field to take down the tent, then they packed everything back on the bike and went to find Stefan. They found him hosing down the parlour while the cows contentedly waited to be released after milking. He was still in good humour, much better than when they had first arrived and they took this to mean that they had not been too much trouble. He waved them off cheerily and like his father, pressed invitations on them to return anytime.

Chapter 14

The route to Paris was straightforward and the weather warm and dry, a perfect day for their trip. The distances on the map were deceptively short but they made good progress following the A13 up towards Deauville and Le Havre then skirting south of Rouen and down to Paris. The journey was so free from traffic they had time to stop for lunch as planned before getting to the Hotel Campanile. They chose a simple omelette followed by a large chocolate gateau to celebrate Martha's birthday then set off again to locate the Hotel in the Paris district. Martha was hoping to have the chance to tidy herself at the Hotel before their encounter with Abigail. The time for this long awaited meeting was suddenly so close she could feel her forehead cold with sweat. She wasn't sure whether it was excitement or fear that was also making her feel quite sick.

Parking the bike outside the Hotel, they agreed to meet at the reception desk after they had both had a chance to freshen up. Martha washed her hands and face in the basin in the ladies room and decided some lipstick might give her some confidence. She brushed her hair and put her jacket over her arm and thought about what she might say. She hoped that Nathalie would have told Abigail a little about her, but then decided she might not have done since Nathalie had told them so little about Abigail's life. Giving herself a final confidant smile in the mirror, she went off to find that Calvin was waiting for her at the Reception desk. She took a deep breath and repeated her brave smile to him then gave the receptionist her name and asked if they could speak to Abigail Ballard.

'You must mean Abigail Piske' the receptionist said. 'She told me to expect a Miss Ballard.' Feeling slightly thrown off balance by this, Martha agreed it must be so. The receptionist smiled encouragingly and pressed connections on a board in front of her. Turning away from the desk, Martha said quietly to Calvin,

'It was probably the name she has always been known by. Monsieur Rombouts told us she was originally brought up on the farm of Monsieur Piske.' Calvin nodded and squeezed her hand. The receptionist replaced the phone and directed them to a room on the next floor. They took the lift in silence and knocked on the door. It was opened by a smartly dressed woman with silvery fair hair and penetrating blue eyes. She was utterly composed and smiled at them with polite curiosity.

'Martha Ballard?' she said as if confirming a reservation and holding out a small, slim hand to shake. 'And you must be Calvin. Come in. We can speak English if you like.' She said over her shoulder in a pleasant and chatty manner. 'I spent many years on reception work at the Hotel and here in Paris it is very necessary to be able to speak English and also German. Please sit down.' They obediently did so and then, feeling quite shy, Martha said,

'I hope we're not intruding?'

'Non, non. You must say what you have come to say.' Martha stared, non-plussed by this directness and looking for signs of recognition or a likeness to herself or her father but she could find none. She had no choice but to start at the beginning.

'My father died in August this year and amongst his papers I found evidence that he was married to Marilor Piske, who I think was your mother. That's right isn't it?'

'That's right.' Martha did not feel she was being helped, but taking a deep breath, she continued.

'I also found a birth certificate for Abigail Ballard.' She paused, again hoping that Abigail would say something. Abigail smiled encouragingly and was more encouraging.

'I guess that's me but I've never seen it. I was too young to worry about what my family name was when I lived at the Farm. Then at the Orphanage, all our legal papers were looked after by the nuns. I actually assumed my name was the same as Hervé and Janine's, which is Gerard. But as soon as I could write, the nuns told me I was to use the name Piske, my mother's name before she was married, so I'm afraid that led me to believe that she had never been legally married. It wasn't the sort of question the nuns encouraged, they would tell us not to worry ourselves about matters which didn't concern us. Most of us had a shadowy background.' She added with a wry smile.

Martha drew out the envelope containing the birth certificate of Abigail and also the marriage certificate between Abigail's mother and her father and held it out to her saying,

'Your mother was definitely married, to my father Jeremiah and this could mean that we are related, I think.' Still showing no sign of the shock that Martha had felt, Abigail took the papers and read them carefully. She didn't seem at all fazed by what she read and she continued politely.

'As I believe you know from Nathalie, it was Jean-Paul who I thought of as my brother and who then told me that Janine and Hervé were not my parents. I think that at the time I was quite glad, because Jean-Paul was a most unpleasant boy in those days and he tried to rape me at the home and as for Janine, I could barely remember her because she never came to see me after I left the farm. By the time I knew she was my aunt, it didn't seem to matter anymore. And this certificate doesn't prove we shared the same father does it?' She smiled ruefully, almost sympathetically as she handed back the documents to Martha. Instead of asking questions about her alleged father or possible sister, Abigail told them about Jean-Paul.

'I hated Jean-Paul for a long time after that, but now I realise that he was a seriously troubled boy. He was frightened of his own sexuality, because you see he was homosexual. To combat this and to prove to the world and also himself that he was heterosexual, he tried to get every girl he met into bed with him. Of course, it didn't make him feel any better and he ended up feeling very guilty and bad about himself. I learned this from his father Hervé, because he used to visit me occasionally, but he never told Janine about his visits or talked about his son being homosexual. It wasn't acceptable in those days and his father was just upset about his son's lack of respect for women. I think he was more than a little afraid of Janine too. He used to call her the original whiplash lady, but he was talking about her tongue.' Abigail laughed at this and the other two smiled and the atmosphere began to relax. Abigail, still smiling said, 'I once asked him why he came to visit me, no-one else did, and he said, maybe I am your father.' Abigail related this calmly and confidently, happier for the moment to talk about other people than about herself. 'So then I asked him about my real mother. He said she was blonde and pretty and that I looked like her. Such a flatterer! But he was also kind and wasn't secretive like everyone else was. He gave me her address at the prison and so I was able to write to her. But it was all too late. She wrote to me just once in return and then after that, Stefan came especially to see me, to tell me she had died. The prison had written to his father who is a solicitor but he apparently had no wish to see me to give me this information. The nuns told me as well, but because I was going to be fourteen, they were more interested in discussing my future than my past.'

'Nathalie told us a little about the Orphanage.' Martha said. 'Were they kind to you?'

'Kind? I think practical would describe them better. Everything was orderly; no wonder they call it an Order! It's very apt I think. They kept us all very busy all the time. When I was fourteen they gave me a lot more freedom. I was even allowed to go out on my own as long as I said where I was going. I think you know from Nathalie that we worked together in the kitchens for a couple more years before I got my first job in a hotel, in the kitchen of course. Nathalie was a sweet person, still is and she taught me well. The hotel was pleased with my work, probably because I was so used to hard work and doing as I was told that I found the work quite easy by comparison with the Orphanage. But I think you want to hear about my mother, is that right?'

'I want to hear about everything!' Martha said.

Sighing a little, Abigail continued. 'After she died, I went to visit the prison in Caen to pick up anything she had owned but really, to see what it was like or if they could tell me anything about her. Well, they weren't really very helpful. They had thrown away any personal things as being of no use or value. I know this wouldn't have been very much anyway, but still, I found that hurtful. She had no contact with family, just the name of the solicitor, Monsieur Rombouts. They told me she saw the Priest every week, more so after she became ill. So I asked if I could see him too. They told me I would have to come back on Wednesday. This was very awkward for me, because I had to go back to the Home and ask for another day off. Because it was a Priest I was going to see, I think the Nuns were more sympathetic! So I went back the following Wednesday and I saw the Priest. He was a kind man, very old in my young eyes but happy to talk about my mother. He said she was very sad, very repentant because of me. I didn't know if he was just being kind and at first I couldn't sympathise with that notion. She hadn't tried to find out what had happened to me as far as I knew. But then, I don't suppose she would have been allowed to. But why had she risked so much? Why also had she disowned me when she came back to the Farm with her sister? The Priest spent quite a time trying to placate me, trying to explain to me that my mother was too full of trust and hope and not able to believe anything bad would come of her friendships. To me, I was young and at an emotional age, she just sounded foolish and selfish.'

'Perhaps to make me feel kinder towards her, he told me a little bit about her life in the prison, which sounded cold and meagre. She had a small cell which she shared and which had bunk beds and a lavatory. They were brought a bowl of cold water every day to wash in. They occasionally had showers which were all open so that the staff could see them and the water was cold with some sort of antiseptic in it. They all had very short hair, not shaven, he told me, because that would have taken too long to do and would have to happen too regularly. Short hair was good enough. Mentally, he said she was constantly depressed, the total opposite of the person I had been told about by Hervé, who was bright, cheery and sociable. She must have been in her late twenties and early thirties when the Priest knew her and he said she looked fifty years old, thin, pale and tired. Apparently none of them slept well because of the noises from the other inmates and the banging around of the guards who took pleasure in making life as unpleasant as possible. She didn't make any friends there; for one thing, it was actively discouraged and for another, the women who were there by now were a different kind of person from Marilor. They were thieves, prostitutes and murderers and she was none of these. In fact she couldn't understand why she was there at all. Why hadn't she been shot, she would ask the Priest, if they think I did wrong. He would repeat to her what he told me, that he thought her innocent of malice, just foolish and misguided. It's hard for me to judge her now, because the law has already judged her and she has paid the price. I have such scant memories of her.'

After this admission to such strong feelings, Abigail's mood abruptly changed. She sat up straighter and asked them, 'Would you like coffee?' They both agreed to accept the perennial French invitation and Abigail switched on a kettle which was in the same room they were in and made them all instant coffee. Looking around them at this impersonal hotel room, they guessed that Abigail lived in just these two rooms, the bedroom opening off this one taking her meals in the restaurant or the Hotel kitchen. Perhaps she also had to give the rooms up for something smaller if they were very busy. They sat with their coffee and biscuits which were individually wrapped, as was the sugar. With renewed composure, Abigail continued.

'As the years have gone by, I have felt sorry for Marilor, but not then, not at that time. The Priest also told me that my mother had a message for me if I should ever come to the prison after her death.' Abigail stopped to look at Martha with a kindly expression. 'He told me my mother had said that my father was a German Officer.'

Martha didn't know whether to laugh or cry. Was she relieved? Glad that her father had not told her about Abigail because he knew she wasn't his? Did she even believe it? Calvin had warned her before they left for France that this was a possibility. She asked the only question she could think of.

'Do you know if it's true? I mean, why did you call yourself Piske and not take the name of the German? If Ballard isn't your name, surely, nor is Piske?'

'I suppose that was because there has always been some doubt about who my father is and so I thought I would take my mother's name, the only one I was sure about.' She looked at Martha sympathetically. 'But I do have a note she wrote to me given to me by the Priest. It has the German Officer's name and his old address. His name was August Mennen and he lived north of Strasbourg in a place called Saarbrucken, Germany.' Looking at her watch, she finished in a rush,

'Look, I'm sorry but I haven't time to talk anymore now, I'm due in the kitchen for my duty roster. Why don't you stay here for your evening meal, then I could join you later for a drink? The hotel isn't very busy tonight and I'm sure I could find you a room for the night as well if you wanted me to?'

Martha was grateful. Her thoughts were slightly chaotic but she had warmed to Abigail while hearing her story. She guessed that it had not been easy for her to talk so intimately about herself to anyone and she didn't want the connection to be broken.

'That would be great, thanks. We'd love to stay, wouldn't we Cal. What time will you be free?'

'I'll meet you both about 9pm, but first, I'll get you a room sorted out at Reception'

Chapter 15

Martha and Calvin were allocated a room and revelled in the luxury of a bath and a comfortable bed. They didn't have anything smart to change in to and settled for clean T-shirts and were thankful for the continued pleasantly warm temperatures. They had a leisurely dinner, foregoing the temptations of a bottle of wine, deciding they should save their wine intake until Abigail joined them later. They were pleasantly surprised when she arrived at their table soon after they had finished eating, carrying three glasses and an opened bottle of red Bordeaux.

After asking if they had enjoyed their meal and pouring them each a generous glass of wine she said,

'I've been thinking. I'm due some leave from the Hotel and you have set me wondering. Would you like to come with me to Germany? Maybe we could locate Monsieur Mennen or should I say, Herr Mennen? Saarbrucken is about four or five hours from here by road, but there is also a train station there. Or perhaps you don't have any more time?'

'That would be wonderful! Actually we have more than another week left, so what do you say Cal?'

'Why not?' He grinned, feeling pleased that Abigail was so comfortable in their company. 'But are you sure about this? You've had the letter from the Priest for a long time and not contacted this German guy. Something must have stopped you from looking into it all. Why now?' Abigail thoughtfully studied the rich dark red of her wine, watching the traces of silky crescents moving down inside the glass before replying.

'Any family I thought I had either left me or denied my existence. To find you have come across the Channel to see if I might be your sister has touched me deeply. I don't know who my father was and therefore I don't know if I have brothers or sisters. I find it very moving that you can so happily accept this as a possibility.' She looked straight into Martha's eyes, 'Perhaps I can also hope that we will stay friends even if we are not related?' Tears burned in Martha's as she covered Abigail's hand with her own.

'I would like that, and I hope so too.'

Abigail turned to Calvin. 'Perhaps it is only now that I have found the need to know the truth.' She stood and embraced them both but was as usual, practical. Her time was more restricted than theirs she said and they agreed they shouldn't waste any more of it than was necessary. She suggested that Calvin and Martha should go to Saarbrucken on the bike and that she, Abigail, would go by train and then meet at the *Hauptbahnhof* in Saarbrucken the next afternoon. Apologising for leaving them so soon, she said she would arrange everything, make some phone calls to check train times and have someone take on her duties in the kitchen. Smiling with evident enjoyment at being able to organise it all, she said she would also try to book them all into a Campanile Hotel in Saarbrucken.

After she had gone, Calvin poured the rest of the wine and they talked about the new direction their plans were taking. They went to bed early in preparation for the next day and Martha's final words to Calvin were, 'Even if she isn't my sister, I really like her.'

Chapter 16

Hans Mennen was married and had three children, Greta, Hans and Karl. His wife was a nurse at the local hospital and he was a sports injury therapist. They lived in Saarbrucken in the house which used to be his father Augusts', but now belonged once again to his grandmother, although she didn't live there with them anymore. His mother was a sad victim of an unspecified nervous condition which had since deteriorated into dementia and the family managed to take care of her in relays. Maria Mennen, Hans' wife worked split shifts and sometimes her duties were at night, sometimes during the day. As Hans had a consultancy room in the house, he could choose his appointments to suit the demands of his wife, his mother and the children.

At that moment, he was sitting in his consultation room thoughtfully studying his nails, which he had to keep immaculately trimmed for his work. He rubbed in a high quality cream while waiting for his visitors. Apart from his hands, he was not a conceited man or overly concerned about his appearance. He had polio as a child and had got used to the isolation that this had caused, being different, walking with a limp and being excluded from some of the more energetic games at school. It was the special attention that he received to help him to walk better that had caught and held his interest sowing the seeds for a future in sports injury therapy. Sports injuries was a slight misnomer because he also worked with all kinds of physical disabilities caused by accidents whether at work or on the road. He had grown up without a father and his mother's condition, now that she was into her seventies had been getting progressively worse. In fact, he had been taking responsibility for her nervous and unstable disposition for years, but it weighed more heavily on him these days, with the children growing up and joining the ranks of those with demands on his time. Fun and enjoyment were nearly always suppressed or rejected by the need to keep his diary full and to provide a comfortable home for his wife and family. They had an acceptable standard of living but he prided himself on being a conscientious and dutiful man and he did not want these values to slip.

He didn't think about the War anymore, not much of it had registered with him anyway and he tried not to think about his father at all. But the phone call he had received last night from Abigail Piske had at least temporarily changed that. Now he was feeling a mixture of annoyance at the intrusion and vague concern as to what these people from France could possibly want to talk to him about. All he really knew was that the woman who phoned originally came from a part of France where his father had been stationed during the War and that the two friends who would accompany her were English. He would make sure his mother was well out of the way when he received his visitors later.

He was certain in his own mind that his father's death in 1945 had tipped his mother's already fragile mind further over the edge. She had longed for his return after his years of absence during the War while stationed in France, so her grief at the news of his death had been nothing short of manic. Hans knew that she had been taken in and protected by her own mother or she would have been admitted to an asylum years ago and never seen again. After her mother's death from a stroke, the responsibility to keep her out of a mental institution had fallen to him.

He knew from occasional more rational conversations about the War years with her and also with his grandmother on his father's side, that it had not been too difficult for her to exchange letters with his father during the time he was away. She had cherished those she received from him, writing back twice as often to keep him up to date with news of himself, their only child. Hans had been just a small baby when his father, a reluctant conscript had left for the War. He knew from his grandmother that his father had been well educated enough to be very quickly promoted to Officer Status in the Wehrmacht. Tall, fair haired and handsome, he was well liked and he traded on his popularity, laughing and joking at the exploits of his fellow officers while keeping his private opinions to himself at a time when stepping out of line was mortally dangerous. He worried about his wife, who was always nervous for his safety and tried to reassure her in his letters of his love and fidelity, without revealing any tales of those of his contemporaries who appeared to have a less active conscience and who were altogether less moral. There were many such tales of sexual exploits and criminal activities by the Wehrmacht, which had been brought to light after the War had ended and vehemently denied thereafter. Most of the accusations concerned particularly officious Officers who had openly encouraged all Nazi protocol and had taken it upon themselves to execute Jews, Poles and gypsies without any pretence of following legal procedures. August Mennen made sure his wife knew nothing of these things, his letters were full of reassurances and love, making his eventual death all the more painful and unacceptable to her. Hans reflected cynically that she had held herself together just long enough to give him her son, a good education and until he was able to take over her care from her mother who had promptly died.

Abigail Piske and her friends had asked to see him to discuss his father's time in the War. Hans was not at all happy about this intrusion into the organised symmetry of his routine and had only reluctantly agreed to see them. He told himself that his reasons for relenting, which even now were against his better judgement were twofold. Firstly, he had some spare time in his diary and secondly, he was curious to know what these people from France and England could possibly want to know about his father, a man who had been dead now for thirty five years.

Chapter 17

Calvin parked his bike at the station and then guided Martha to the waiting room at Saarbrucken Station where they had agreed to meet Abigail. She was there already, flipping through a magazine. She told them of her success in finding the telephone number of Herr Mennen, who was still living at the same address she had been given by the Priest and that Herr Hans Mennen, son of August Mennen would see them at his address at 3.30pm. He told her it would be easy to find as it was also a Therapy Centre for sports injuries, clearly marked on the door. Not having brought a town map with them, they decided to hire one of the Mercedes taxis parked outside the station. They sat, each within their own thoughts during the drive, only speaking to agree that Abigail should be their spokesperson. They had no idea how long the taxi journey would take and as it turned out, they arrived at least an hour early.

Having established the exact location, they agreed to walk to a near-by coffee house and relax for a while and recover from their early morning start. Abigail expanded further on the telephone call she had made to Herr Mennen. She had found his number quite easily she told them, on the Hotel computer which had telephone books stored for many European countries. Knowing the name of his hometown and also his address had made it simpler as there were very few Mennens listed in the town of Saarbrucken. Herr Mennen had answered the telephone himself and she had been able to quickly establish that his first name was Hans and yes, he was the son of the Officer, August Mennen who her mother had known in France. She related what Hans had told her, that August Mennen had died soon after his return to Germany, but she said that Hans had not elaborated on the cause of his death and she had thought it might alienate him if she asked him for more details. She thought it would be best to meet him where they could ask him face to face.

Changing the subject she then went on to tell them about her train trip, which had taken her on a direct link from Paris East to Saarbrucken in four and a half hours and how much she had admired the beautiful rolling countryside. She said with a smile, that if she hadn't been so nervous at the outcome of their quest she would have enjoyed it more. But it had been quite relaxing even so. They were impressed by her calm pragmatism and told her so. Almost reluctantly and each wondering what the outcome would be, they walked back to the Therapy Centre.

Chapter 18

They could not have known from his appearance just how nervous Hans Mennen was also feeling. His social skills were usually only called upon in a professional sphere and he and his wife were not in the habit of forming friendships. To them, life seemed to be quite busy and complicated enough already. Buttoning up his jacket which he had worn in place of the white coat he would normally wear and masking his feelings behind a bland, polite exterior, he opened the door to his visitors.

Introductions were formally made but no explanations were offered at this stage as to who everyone was or might be. As agreed, they left all the talking to Abigail, as her German was impeccable compared with theirs, which was basic and inadequate. They were shown into a room lined with books and which was furnished with several chairs and a large desk as well as other paraphernalia connected with the running of an office. Hans sat down behind the desk where normally he would have taken down notes and information from his clients. He did this unconsciously but it lent him some authority, sending a message to them of having the advantage and of being in charge, when in fact he felt the reverse. This rather obvious tactic faintly amused Abigail and had the opposite effect on her, helping her to feel more confidant.

She took the lead, explaining where she had lived and a short history of the circumstances of her enforced stay in the Orphanage. Hans listened silently, regarding her politely, though looking tense as she also told him about her mother and the circumstances of her death. Her composure slipped a little as Hans's coldness began to affect her. She continued as briefly as she could, telling the story right up to her meeting with Martha and Calvin who she indicated with a smile and a wave of her hand. Hans nodded briefly at them and taking this as a slightly encouraging sign, she then told him about the Priest and the message he had delivered from her mother and his words to her concerning Herr August Mennen.

At this point, Hans held up his hand, almost physically warding off anything further from her. He appeared to be choosing his words carefully and spoke slowly as if keeping himself in check and indeed, his voice shook slightly.

'This is a lot to take in, and first I must tell you that my mother is here in this house. She is ill, she doesn't understand very much and I can never mention my father to her without her becoming very distressed. It was always that way, but since the dementia she now has, it is much worse, so I will not ask her anything at all. In the early years I would ask questions, but it was my grandmother who told me the truth about my father.'

'The truth?' said Martha. Ignoring her, he continued.

'You know I believe that my father is dead?' They all nodded solemnly. 'He was shot dead on his arrival here in Germany after the War, as a traitor. Not as you might imagine,' he said, glaring at Abigail, 'as a rapist or for fathering an illegitimate child, Madame Piske, no, as a traitor. I don't believe for one minute that he is your father as you are implying. The idea is absurd, preposterous and frankly, insulting. His letters to my mother would belie any possibility of that. They had not been married for more than a year or so before he was conscripted into the Wehrmacht and from all that she has ever told me, they were very much in love.' He sat up straighter in his chair.

'I realise that you will think this is hard for me to know, since I have absolutely no recollections of him myself and would in any case, have been far too young to be any judge of character. But my grandmother also spoke of him when I was old enough to ask questions. Sadly, she is now dead.'

Abigail spoke soothingly. 'We have no wish to upset you Herr Mennen, or your mother. If this is all too painful for you, we will leave now. Perhaps I have been thoughtless and carried along with the enthusiasm of my English friends here and if so I apologise. We didn't know these were unhealed wounds, it was all so long ago.'

Herr Mennen looked mollified at this unequivocal apology.

'As you have come so far, I will tell you how it really was so that you can understand because I am not ashamed of what he did. My parents lived here in this house, the family house on my father's side going back several generations and as you know from your journey here, we are quite close to the French border. My father had a cousin who lived in Strasbourg. His family were isolated there after the city was claimed once again from Germany by the French after World War 1. The whole family had to learn both French and German and my father spent many months of his youth there on holidays and so forth. He was an only child and the two cousins were like brothers. They both learned to speak each others' language fluently through this association. Strasbourg was again occupied for several years during the Second World War and although I'm not sure of any of the details of where my uncle went but my father must have kept in touch with him because this connection along with the one with your mother, Marilor Piske,' here he nodded at Abigail, 'and some fool of a young Englishman who is your father, I presume,' he said, turning to Martha, 'is why my father was shot as a traitor.' Hans Mennen regarded each one of them with an accusing expression of ill-disguised exasperation and anger.

His voice, which had been rising steadily with his words, now dropped again as he continued more calmly.

'He was allowed to see his mother before the execution but my own mother, his wife, was too distraught at the knowledge of what was about to happen to him and had already gone to pieces. They wouldn't let her near him with her hysterics. So it was my grandmother who saw him before the execution and it was she who told me what he had said. She didn't want me to think my father was a bad man, which is how she thought my mother would see him. The truth is that through the gossipy words of Marilor Piske, he discovered the undercover plans of the Englishman. However, my father didn't use this information **against** the English, he used it to help them. His Strasbourg cousin was part of an underground ante Nazi movement positioned on the northern beaches of France who helped English, Canadians, Polish and even some Jews to get back to England. My father was a part of this operation. They were both pacifists at heart, as well as being French sympathisers and were aghast at the stringent measures taken against Jews in particular by the Nazis and the Gestapo and so zealously backed up by the Wehrmacht. It appears that several of my father's fellow officers were not unaware of his sympathies and were even suspicious of his relationship with your mother, not accepting that it was just a flirtation. He encouraged the belief that he was having an affair with her but his aim was solely to discover information and to pass it on to his French cousin. So you see, he can't be your father. My grandmother doesn't believe that he was unfaithful to his wife, despite the fact that she doesn't like her.'

Martha had been following quite a lot of this but not all, and Abigail occasionally stopped to interpret for them. But now Martha had a question,

'Can you ask him how it was that your mother was arrested in France and he wasn't?' Hans understood the question and answered straight away.

'That was because her own countrymen turned her in. At that time, my father's double deceit wasn't known.'

'So that would have been Janine.' Abigail said.

'I don't know who Janine is,' Hans replied, 'but I know that there was another man involved, because he was also instrumental in getting my father arrested. It was a Monsieur Rombouts.'

Chapter 19

At that moment, the door was flung open and a heavily built, wild eyed woman stumbled erratically into the room brandishing a very large kitchen knife. They all turned to stare in astonishment at the intruder.

'I saw you come here!' Hans' mother yelled at them, for that was who she was. 'I've been listening. Get out, you French cow.' She said this, turning to Abigail, the knife raised ready to strike. Hans stood up quickly, upsetting his chair but staying firmly behind the table, he shouted at her.

'Stop! Go back to your room mother!' And then, panic rising in his voice, he yelled to his wife.

'Maria, come quickly.' Calvin jumped up from behind Frau Mennen and reached over her head for the knife, but he was not quick enough and she had already brought it down on Abigail's shoulder. Martha also leapt to her feet and while Calvin struggled to retrieve the knife, she faced the woman and slapped her hard across the face. This effectively stopped her, just as Maria hurried into the room.

'She said she was getting a glass of water!' Maria exclaimed, as if trying to stop anyone allocating blame right away. Glaring at her mother-in-law, she took a firm hold on her arm and led her away, still grumbling.

'She must have been listening all the time.' She continued to pull her through the door and along a dark corridor into the kitchen and Calvin followed behind still holding the knife. He placed it as far away as possible from Frau Mennen senior as he could while Maria took some pills from a locked cabinet, shaking out two or three from the bottle.

'These are sedatives, it's all I can do for her,' she said, pushing the other woman down into a chair and watching over her as she swallowed the pills using the neglected glass of water still standing on the table. Calvin felt there was nothing he could add to this so he turned away and walked back to the office to check on his two companions.

Martha leaned over to look at Abigail's shoulder. The blade had slipped under the thick lapel and cut the cloth under the collar but fortunately it hadn't penetrated her skin.

'She should be locked up!' she said furiously.

'I'm fine, Martha. Really, I'm not hurt.'

For the first time, Hans looked vulnerable and shaken and apologising for nearly bumping into Calvin as he was returning, he hurried out in the direction of his wife in the kitchen, happy to escape and saying he would get them all a drink. He returned quickly with a tray carrying a bottle of brandy but with only three glasses which he filled with an unsteady hand.

'She's getting worse. My wife is giving her a sedative, she'll have a sleep I expect. Please accept my apologies, I was afraid something like this might happen, anything to do with my father, you know.' His words came out jerkily, nervous and defensive now and evidently anxious for them to leave, he continued.

'Look, perhaps you could talk to my grandmother, Frau Mennen, she lives in a retirement apartment just round the corner, just two streets away. I'll give you the address and phone number and I'll tell her what you have told me. I'm sorry but I really think you had better leave.' He didn't have a drink himself and remained standing as they sipped the brandy, transparently willing them to go as soon as possible.

Obediently putting their glasses back on the tray, they filed outside the house where they stood huddled as if it was cold, Calvin clutching the piece of paper with the address and Martha in turn, clutching Abigail.

'Oh my God!' said Martha in a dazed voice. 'I don't believe that just happened!'

Abigail, forever practical and recovering swiftly suggested they find a taxi to take them to the Hotel where she had booked them two rooms. 'I can't face another meeting like that one today. I'll phone the grandmother from the hotel and hope she can see us tomorrow.

Abigail was greeted very respectfully at the Hotel and Martha found herself wondering how much of this was due to Abigail's position in the Paris Hotel or simply to staff loyalty. They were shown to their rooms and offered a private sitting room and an aperitif before ordering dinner. She was beginning to suspect that Abigail was a lot more than just someone who worked in the kitchen since nothing was too much trouble for them. They ordered their meal, staying with an authentic German menu of frankfurters, sauerkraut and potatoes followed by hot apple strudel and cream. They couldn't help but talk over the events of the afternoon and Martha voiced what they were all thinking.

'Wasn't that awful? And I didn't like Hans one bit. I do hope you're not related to him.' Martha said and Calvin added his opinion.

'He didn't want you to be did he? It was like there were things he knew but he had stored it all away, never to be looked at again. I suppose that was because of his mother, because she was seriously deranged! But there must be some doubts in his mind or he wouldn't have agreed to see you, Abigail. I hope the grandmother is going to be a bit more human. It's a good job we didn't meet the kids, they were probably like something out of 'The Munsters."

They laughed and then Abigail said it was getting late and she ought to phone Frau Mennen and try to arrange a meeting. She hoped that Hans would have paved the way for their visit. She returned after five minutes and said yes, it was settled, they would go there tomorrow at 10 in the morning.

'I think she's a bit deaf but otherwise she sounded quite pleasant. We shall see. I think I'm going to bed now, it's been a very long day. See you at breakfast?'

Calvin and Martha decided to take a look at the Bar and have a drink before bed. It was quite busy and they felt a little out of place amongst the other guests who looked like business people, so they found a quiet table and drank their beers.

'You know, Abigail could have some DNA checks run, for instance to find out if she is related to me. If she wanted to,' she added.

'Can they do that?'

'Well, we'd probably have to pay and it's not as conclusive as it would be between a father and daughter. But I've read about it and as a science it's progressed a lot in the last few years. I think it's about matching a number of strands so if neither of us had any strands in common, then the likelihood would be that we aren't related, but if on the other hand, there were some matches then the only conclusion they could come to would be that we shared the same father, as he is the only relative we would have in common.'

'D'you think she would agree?'

'I think that now she has met the horrible Hans, she might be less eager to accept him as her brother, don't you? Perhaps confirmation would be the last thing she would want.'

'You've got a point and I can't see him having a test done.'

They found their room on the same floor as Abigail's and snuggled down under the duvet facing each other. Calvin stroked her hair away from her eyes.

'Are you OK?'

'Course I am. If Abigail can cope, so can I. But it has been weird hasn't it? And what about Hans saying it was Monsieur Rombouts who spilled the beans about Marilor? D'you believe that?'

'They seemed such a nice couple and he told us he didn't know what was going on at the time.'

'Yes, But he knew afterwards didn't he.'

'Stefan doesn't have a very good relationship with him, does he?'

'What about Madame Rombouts?'

'Well. We didn't really get to know her did we? She was ill in the War and now she just seems like the domestic goddess without the usual endowments.' Martha giggled at this.

'D'you think you could ever be a domestic goddess?' Teasing and snuggling closer, Martha replied.

'Would you want me to be?'

'I think I'd quite like us to have children. We could hire a cook.'

'I can cook! Can you? And how many kids would you want?'

'Three sets of twins.' Laughing and instinctively shying away from any more serious conversation, they made love instead.

The next morning, they met Abigail in the Breakfast Bar where Calvin proceeded to load a tray with every sort of breakfast combination from across Europe while Martha found a table for three. Abigail greeted them each with a kiss and they sat down to enjoy the variety Calvin had selected for them.

Chapter 20

Madame Rombouts, Sylvie in her younger persona, had never been a pretty woman, her charms were simple ones. As a young woman she had shiny though mousy coloured hair, a slim figure, inclined to be top heavy, a pleasant face but unremarkable. She had a pleasingly positive personality with average intelligence and a penchant for making things. When Henri Rombouts met her he liked the fact that she didn't attract too much interest and that she had an acquiescent personality, not a girl who would argue. There weren't a lot of girls to choose from, but it would be harsh to say she was the best of a bad lot. Henri on the other hand, was accepted as being a good catch. He was neatly built and dark haired with a handsome face which reflected a personality determined to succeed though not in any way ruthless. His parents had encouraged his continued education through lycée and college, acquiring his Baccalaureate and going on to study law. He was not a lawyer but a *notaire* or solicitor which gave him a certain status in the eyes of villagers and also a choice of potential girlfriends. He met and married Sylvie who was impressionable and grateful for his attentions.

They were both born before the beginning of the First World War which had brought devastation to both their families, killing fathers and brothers and cousins, enough to leave them affected by War even though neither had real memories of experiencing it at firsthand. Sylvie was a person who was accepting rather than critical, modest enough to know she couldn't change a person unless it was their wish. Henri, in his profession found that he often had to change the minds of others in order to resolve a problem and had grown used to the concept of changing other people's minds for them. In this way, he became something of a bully and thought his brain and opinions superior to those of others, including his wife. She didn't appear to mind this, holding him in such high regard. Her role in life was to be creative: sewing, gardening, baking, bottling and preserving and also of course, making babies. Stefan was born in 1936, the first of many she hoped for, but instead of revelling in his babyhood she became obsessed with the desire for another child, sure in her mind that lots of children made an ideal family. Unfortunately she did not conceive again so easily and when finally she did, she miscarried mid-term. This was followed by a series of pregnancies and miscarriages all through the second War, leaving her weak and unwell and very depressed.

Henri was not a sympathetic partner to her sad difficulties, he was rather the reverse. He browbeat his wife into carrying on with her household chores which he had come to rely on as his right and taunted her with her inadequacies, insensitive to the affect he was having on her depression. As a young man whose profession and connections to the Government exempted him from fighting, he let it be known that his position was more important than her or the child. But Sylvie was not going to let his attitude crush her, she overcame his overbearing manners with a pleasant and cheery smile and fought her depression with more pregnancies until the end of the War when she finally carried Michel to full term.

During those years of disruption and chaos, Henri Rombouts had his own reasons for being less than sympathetic to his wife's condition as he was kept very busy man with his own agenda. In fact he admired her ability to carry on through all the pain and distress with such a brave face because his own situation was causing him anxiety which he found a strain to conceal. He knew of Marilor's association with a German Officer and he also knew her reputation. Jeremiah Ballard had been welcomed as a friend at his home and on the eve of his final day in France he had hinted at the rescues and failures with which he had been involved and that Marilor was not backing him up in this. After Jeremiah had left, Henri was determined to find out what Marilor was doing and if she really did have a part in any of Jeremiah's schemes. He had to be patient and wait until after her return from her sister Janice, now with two children and then he systematically set about gaining her trust. He planned coincidences where he could meet Marilor in the Bar/Tabac or on the way to the town and then took the opportunity to flirt charmingly with her, before he finally asked her to meet him at his office in the town. Their meetings had become regular and intimate and there were times for Henri when he wasn't sure whether the enticement of Marilor's pretty face and lovely body were more important than his self imposed task. Her body was certainly more exciting and interesting to him than his wife's.

In those years after Jeremiah had left Henri learned many things about himself and those around him, complicated information which he found hard to live with. He could be disloyal, he could lie, and he could bully and deceive. He could be unfaithful to his wife and Marilor was the most excitingly sexual being he had ever had the pleasure of encountering. Their love making was always rapid and conspiratorial and left him disturbed both mentally and physically. Totally distracted from his purpose, he found it difficult to ask her such mundane questions as who she talked to in the German Camp or what she said. He discovered that these questions stuck in his throat which had self sealed with jealousy. His discoveries regarding collaborators were small fry and commonplace compared with his liaisons with Marilor, but he passed them on to his contact in the government anyway.

Chapter 21

Frau Gertrud Mennen, mother of August and grandmother to Hans, was twisting her long silver hair into a simple knot on top of her head which she then secured with a large black headed pin. She was grateful that she could still reach her hands over her head at her age. Getting old was no fun she thought, picking up a mirror to check the back of her hair. She had been wearing it like this for so many years she found it easy to do now. In her days as a dancer it had been a style they had all adopted.

She wanted to look her best for her visitors and so she chose a fine woollen black dress to wear with a cross over front which then fell to a slim skirt. She picked up a mahogany cane with a large rounded silver top which nestled warmly into her hand and walked carefully over to a full length mirror to view the effect. She gave her reflection a satisfied nod. Though not fashionable the dress suited her perfectly and she looked elegant for all her ninety years.

She sat down on the bed and reflected on the phone calls she had received from both her son Hans, sounding distraught and agitated and then the French woman who called herself Abigail Piske. She had recognised the name Piske at once but she had never heard the two names put together before. Hearing it again had taken her right back, further even than the events these people were so keen to talk to her about.

She thought about Hans' father August, the subject of her visitors' interest and how he had so rarely seen his son. History had cruelly repeated itself because her husband Karl had not lived to see their son August, and for the same reason, because War had killed both the father and the son. Different Wars but the same brutality. She had met Karl in Berlin where she had gone with a dancing troupe. Berlin, she sighed nostalgically, with its bright cafés filled with young people interested in the arts, culture and fun. Karl was a trumpet player and she thought of him now for the first time for many years. She remembered the lock of hair that would flop onto his forehead when he pressed the trumpet's mouthpiece to his lips and how she would admire the muscles moving in his strong hands when he fingered the buttons. She could almost hear the music, the tempo already starting to reflect an awakening interest in jazz at that time. They had been so in love, they had cut short their courtship and married after just a few months. They lived with his parents and his sisters in Berlin and then when she became pregnant and was no longer able to dance, his family were happy for her to stay with them and to be there to welcome their first grandchild. She got on well with his sisters, having none of her own.

Her son, August was born in August of 1914 and by then, World War One was already upon them. It had all happened with astonishing speed. Franz Joseph, King of Austria and Hungary and a mighty power of the Hapsburg dynasty had suffered several irritations from Serbia. But when Emperor Franz Ferdinand, his nephew and the heir to the throne had been murdered in Sarajevo by a Serbian agitator along with his pregnant wife, then this he could not ignore. He declared his country to be at War with Serbia and called upon his allies which included Germany and Italy, the Triple Alliance. Russia and France along with the UK were allied with Serbia, the Triple Entente. These mighty powers of Europe, several of which had already changed sides since 1882 looked upon the Serbian uprising as an opportunity to redress the balance of power in Europe and an opportunity to call upon the loyalty of allies to regain lost territories.

Millions had died in that most terrible of Wars, horrifying statistics which came to light afterwards. 200,000 alone had died in the rat infested, disease ridden trenches. The numbers of those who had suffered scars which they would carry with them for the rest of their lives were not included. 11% of France's population had also been either killed or wounded. It had been an infected wound which had killed her beloved Karl, a fact which she had not found out until much later. He would never see his son, a small insignificant statistic amidst the global madness of it all. At the time, the repercussions were undreamed of.

After the sad day that Karl had left to fight, Gertrud fully expected him to be back by her side for the birth of their baby in a few months. His sister Hilde had gone to Strasbourg to marry her beau, and the other sister, Dana was still at home with her parents and was by then a doting aunt to August.

Gertrud Mennen sat with her hands folded in her lap and her head bowed as if in prayer, remembering. Of course, then as always, she had pulled herself together and made the best of her life. She and her son had stayed with Karl's family until the end of the War. Travelling was not easy in those days of requisitioning anything that moved on wheels and she had put off any ideas of returning home to her parents. America had joined the War effort in 1917 to help put an end to the madness that had swept through Europe, just before it had nearly all burned itself out. After that, she had taken her son who was by then five years old, to meet her parents in the family home in Saarbrucken, with promises to return with him frequently to Berlin to visit Karl's parents. Promises became wishes and these in turn were not often compounded. Her parents welcomed her back and for a while she was able to reclaim a kind of normality into her life, returning to dancing while her parents helped with the care of her son.

Gertrud Mennen took her cane and went into the kitchen of her neat apartment. She had four rooms, a bedroom, bathroom, kitchen and sitting room all on the ground floor and quite large. It was perfectly adequate she felt and she was glad she no longer lived with her grandson, despite the fact that the house he occupied still belonged to her. In her opinion the children were too noisy, her daughter-in-law was a poor, tortured and anguished nightmare of a woman and her grandson's wife was a hard faced person with no artistry, too self occupied to even smile. Gertrud's background as a dancer, her friends and her way of life which had been verging on Bohemian was a fact which she knew offended her narrow minded granddaughter-in-law. She felt sorry for them all, because, despite having lived through two wars which had personally given her so much sorrow, she felt that she at least had the ability to recognise kindness and happiness and culture, all of which were evidently lacking in the lives of her grandson's family. In her mind she glossed over any opinion of her grandson, seeing only his mother in his faults and any good points she attributed to his father.

She had become used to widowhood, as had many thousands across the world after the War but music and dance kept her mind and her feet busy and was also a social outlet for her. Joining a dance troupe again had helped her but she recognised that had she still been married, taking up dancing again might not have been quite so easy. She had been with a company which didn't take her away for too long or too far. Her parents had always encouraged her opinionated and strong minded individuality and benignly tolerated her engagements away from home, happy to look after August in the big house in Saarbrucken. He often spent holidays in Strasbourg where Gertrud went as well, to perform in concerts and stay with Karl's sister. Her nephew Philippe and August were of similar age and played together well. August was acquiring a well rounded education with the attention of so many adults. He was an intelligent, likeable boy, handsome like his mother, sensitive like his father. Gertrud enjoyed their trips to Strasbourg because she had met a man there whom she liked. Not in the least like Karl to look at, he was French and had a great sense of humour. He played the accordion and sang in clubs in the evenings and helped in a bakery at night, going there straight after these engagements, then he would sleep until midday. Wounds from the First World War had led to his leg being amputated but he coped well and accepted Gertrud's frequent absences stoically as he did everything else. There were plenty worse off than he and unlike so many thousands at least he was alive. His outlook on life was optimistic and positive and it was his light hearted, easy going approach to life which appealed to Gertrud.

For many, the fear and suspicion of a Second World War had been building in momentum for several years, but few could believe that anything so bad could happen again. Surely no-one in their right mind would contemplate a repeat of those terrible years. But thoughts of unfinished business stirred in Hitler's breast and the opportunity to dominate the world drove his ambitions. His insane dream was of conquering the World and putting Germany in charge of an Aryan master race. In her forthright manner, Gertrud told her parents that she didn't like this histrionic and despotic man, but already it had become unsafe to voice such strong opinions that were so clearly against the Government. This fuelled her dislike of him and his politics even more and she was deeply angered and frustrated when the news of War broke out in 1939, very much afraid that her son August, at the age of twenty five was the perfect age for recruiting into Hitler's Army.

August had married Sofia the year before and their son Hans was born just at the outbreak of War. The pregnancy had not been an easy one, with sickness throughout the whole term. Sofia had frequently taken to her bed and had put on far too much weight. She slept badly and didn't exercise enough which made the birth more difficult than it needed to have been. She was displaying an unstable state of mind which hitherto had only manifested itself to August as charming, feminine frailty. While she was pregnant, she had been convinced that the baby was dead in her womb and when this proved to be wrong and she delivered a healthy baby boy, she fretted incessantly over him thinking he would die in his cot. She constantly checked his breathing all through the day and the night and consequently she was herself fractious and always tired. Gertrud remembered these times with impatience and very little sympathy. She was glad that Sofia's mother bore the brunt of her daughter's behaviour and was sympathetic to her son when he despaired of pleasing his wife.

Chapter 22

The banging at the door to her apartment brought her into the present and she focused her mind on the meeting ahead. Taking her cane, as much for comfort as for support, she made her way slowly to the door. The group in front of her looked politely expectant and she studied each of the faces in front of her before opening the door wide enough for them to enter. They shook hands in the small hallway, each introducing themselves before following Gertrud into the sitting room.

The room was comfortably furnished with a pleasing blend of colours, pale blues and dark cream. There were several paintings on the walls of dancers and musicians, all originals and tastefully displayed. There were thick plain wool rugs of toning pale blue on a wooden parquet floor. The whole effect was light and tasteful despite some heavy, dark furniture which provided a contrast. Frau Mennen chose a high backed chair and leaned her cane against the seat. Calvin pulled his chair around so they could all see one and other and they waited respectfully for Frau Mennen to speak.

'Please call me Gertrud and I shall call you by your first names if that is all right?' She didn't wait for an answer and carried on. 'I heard there was trouble at my grandson's home yesterday, are you feeling better now?' She looked at Abigail who nodded her reply.

'Yes thank you. Your daughter-in-law must be a great worry to the family?'

'A trial indeed, to my grandson and my son before that. I suppose you could say that Sofia was the cause of my son's infidelity but that would be unfair. We must each answer to our own conscience and not blame others for what should always finally be our own decisions.' To Martha, this sounded like a barely disguised allusion to a great many possibilities, but it was Calvin as usual who jumped in.

'How d'you mean?'

'What I mean, Calvin, is that my son is not here to answer your questions, accusations or whatever they may be, but ultimately, he had a brain, he used it and he made his own decisions, which I admire in anyone.' The sharpness of her words were completely off-set by the disarming smile which accompanied them.

'I felt a great responsibility towards his education and his life in general without a father. He was born right at the beginning of the First World War in Berlin and he never saw his father or my parents until he was five years old. When War broke out, Karl and all his friends in the brass band he played in, they all agreed to join the War, fighting for heaven knew what because patriotism and duty to one's country had not really ever been brought into question or tested by any except the military in those days. No-one could have envisaged the horror of it. Scavenging birds have got more sense, you clap your hands and they're gone. Man does not have the same sense it seems, continuing blindly down the same wrong road, clinging stubbornly to a false belief that if they should win, everything in life will be better. War improves nothing, wouldn't you agree?' She stopped to look at them all, again holding her cane, as if ready to leave if they did not.

Abigail nodded. 'But people worry about who is ruling over them, don't they?' Ignoring this, Gertrud continued.

'Women set great store by relationships and so for this reason, they don't understand war, because war ignores such basic humanitarian feelings and destroys families. And yet, when young men are herded together and find themselves under great stress, as in a combat situation, they start to bond and then they understand about this interaction because they are experiencing it at last. But by then it's too late.'

Abigail responded again. 'You're right, I'm sure. When women cry, men sometimes dismiss it as weakness, feminine affectation or sentiment. Perhaps they cannot see that women weep for love until they learn to weep themselves.'

Calvin fidgeted in his seat; as the only male present he was determined to have his say but he was not in the habit of analysing other people's emotions and especially not in war conditions of which he had no experience.

'Not all men and not all women are the same. Men are also builders and inventors, engineers as well as poets and artists. I suppose a major difference could be that men still believe in actions over words to settle differences. But isn't it difference that makes a world, isn't a country the sum of its parts, all of them?'

Martha took up the challenge. She was enjoying this discussion, even though she found it surprising that this mix of people who hardly knew each other could be so freely airing their views. Gertrud had an authoritative presence and was obviously interested in what they all thought. Martha already admired her and was also feeling more at home with voicing her opinions now that everyone else had done so.

'That may be so in an ideal world, but all the time there is a dictatorship in government or an excessively powerful personality in control, then democracy and decency take a back seat, because these men believe that borders and power are more important than humanity and life. They say they are fighting for freedom, with the good of the country in view, but what they do to achieve this, I believe is a degradation of the human soul.'

Gertrud nodded, saying, 'Strong words, my dear, but I'm glad you feel like that, it's interesting to hear your views since none of you have experienced a war at first hand. Even you Abigail were just a small child and it's good to have a discussion about such things. It may help you to understand what happened to my son.' She then went on to explain and continued with her journey into the past.

'During the First World War and after Karl had died, his family were good to me and to August. I regretted not having more children from his point of view but then, I had a great many things to regret. I had lost my husband and my career by then and very nearly lost touch with my parents because of the War. I tried to make up for those losses after it was over. We were living with my parents but we visited Augusts' cousin, Karl's sister's son in Strasbourg because I sometimes had work there, and this brought the two boys closer. As an only child, it was good for August to have someone his own age to relate to.'

Gertrud paused again, reflecting. 'There were so many single mothers and so many single children in those days. I had hoped August might be musical like his father and I. Then I hoped he might do well at the College of Fine Arts in Saar, but his interests were more down to earth than that and he chose a University in Bonn where he studied Civil Engineering.'

Gertrud stopped again to take a sip of water from the jug she had placed there earlier and then offered them all a glass.

'It must have been hard for you.' Martha said sympathetically.

'Being single? It was no more difficult for me than it was for everyone. I can't say whether life gets easier or we just get more used to bad things happening. So many people died in that War. Sometimes I am ashamed to be German, we were so heavily involved in both Wars, but then every European nation has its own cross to bear, it just depends on their point of view and their beliefs, don't you think?'

'I suppose so. But dominance of one kind or another was what they all wanted, wasn't it? And the result was that families were torn apart and ordinary values changed.'

Abigail spoke again, saying 'I believe you are right, everyone was guilty if they wanted power over others. How strong do your beliefs have to be before you're prepared to kill for them as well as die for them? Hitler hated Jews because he was afraid of their power and he hated all manner of other people as well, for different reasons. Yet he was supposed to be a religious person and therefore, he should surely have been able to accept the imperfections of the human race, but he didn't did he. If you only believe in your own point of view, doesn't that lead to meglo-mania? Does anyone have the right to press their beliefs onto others? Whether they are religious beliefs or personal ones and whether or not you think you are the better person, the better intellect or the better race?'

'Perhaps that is where religion gives some of the answers. It stands in judgement of your beliefs or actions being right or wrong,' said Martha.

'Well it didn't work that way for Hitler did it! Also not all religions believe in the same form of justice or reprisal. The cutting off of the hand that steals, stoning a woman for infidelity even if in fact she was raped. Different religions take a great many beliefs and turn them around to suit their own political views. The swastika was once a sign of peace. It was distorted by Hitler. The cross is an instrument of torture, how many people think about that when they wear it around their necks? Hitler was mad, I think that's one safe assumption and hopefully, that madness would be recognised today as such and not given credence.' Gertrud said. 'War overturns the natural order of things. We are brought up not to kill, then War happens and deserters and pacifists are killed or imprisoned for not wanting to kill and be part of it. Are they cowards or moral heroes?'

Her face shrank into the folds of the ancient as she considered this vexing question, clearly a question that was at the heart of this discussion for her. Her paper-thin skin, pale and crumpled, contrasted with the still blue gaze she cast around. The question hung rhetorically in the air and sensing her weariness, Calvin took the opportunity to ask to use the bathroom. The mood was instantly dispelled and Gertrud stood up to show him the way and also excused herself, saying she would make them all coffee.

On his return, Calvin lingered in the little hallway to look at the photos on the shelf. He picked one up, studying the mother and son it depicted. The mother was an image of Gertrud as a young woman, her hairstyle was the same and the clothes were those worn in the 1920's. The boy must have been her son August and he realised with a shock of recognition that Abigail was the image of him; he could only be her father and Gertrud must have known this as soon as she had seen Abigail in the hallway where he now stood. At that moment Gertrud came out of the kitchen with a tray laden with cups and biscuits. Hastily replacing the photo he hurried towards her to take the tray, raising his slim dark eyebrows in a question. She thrust the tray at him enabling her to put her finger to her lips, the age-old mime for silence. Turning to collect her cane, she hustled him wordlessly back into the lounge.

Calvin carried the tray to a small table and put it down and Martha stood ready to distribute coffee and biscuits. When they were all settled, Gertrud again took up her story, more forthright now and not exactly where she had left off.

'My grandson's mother is a fool, a self-deluding one at that. She is to be looked upon with compassion, though I find my patience and sympathy for her has worn a little thin over the years. She's not a happy woman and never was. A wasted life and I'm truly sorry for her behaviour towards you, she is best kept in her room and out of harm's way. I remember during the War, my son would come home for visits. She would greet him with hysterics, a mixture of effusive hugs followed by accusations of not visiting sooner or writing enough. This was not the gentle teasing of a wife I can assure you, it was nerve wracking for him and for anyone else to witness. She inundated him with her worries about everything and especially her concerns for Hans. Life was hard enough without her making it worse with her weeping and complaining. He did his best to pacify and comfort her but I believe she had a significant mental problem before she was pregnant and having the baby and this enforced separation due to the War just made it worse.'

'Frau Mennen, Gertrud, please could you bear to tell us what happened to your son?' Martha pressed gently. Gertrud looked at each of them as if assessing how they would receive her.

'We have discussed attitudes to War, and I have lived through two. War is an atrocity, an affront to civilisation in my view. My son shared those beliefs. You must also understand that his closest friend, his cousin, was born a Frenchman and so at a time of War, he would therefore be on the opposing side. He too shared the beliefs of my son August. Philippe joined the Legion Françoise de la Revolution National and was posted on the northern beaches of France. He was one of many brave young men who took care of escaping British Airmen. Some of these would have been known to your father, Jeremiah. What your father did not know was that August supplied some of the information which helped these men to safety. I understand your father ferried them down the river Dives in his boat. He was wise to leave France when he did, although I think he would have been recalled by his country anyway, to help continue the fight from his natural country, England. What happened to him Martha?'

'He was one of the lucky ones. He obviously got back home safely, because he joined the RAF and then stayed in the Service until the death of his wife, Abigail's mother in 1955. Then he married my mother. Sadly they are both dead now, my father died just a month ago, from cancer.'

'I'm sorry to hear that, but at least it wasn't the War which took them. The activities of my son and his cousin were few and even fewer after your father left, because the Wehrmacht were hostile and vigilant, rigorous in their pursuit of their Nazi ideals. They would shoot traitors or anyone who deviated from the rules, without a trial. Sadly, their behaviour was a lot more to do with wielding power than any ideas of purifying the race. August hated it and concealed his true beliefs behind his usual easy charm to throw them of the scent. He was not a coward, nor in my view, a traitor because he believed in life and justice, not War. A worthy belief. He befriended Marilor, your mother, Abigail, it is true and he hid behind this friendship to find out the plans being discussed by Jeremiah and some other young men from the cafe. But it was information he passed to his cousin not to the Germans. So yes, he was a traitor to Hitler. I'm sorry to say that, but yes, he also duped Marilor by seducing her and she became pregnant very early on in the War. Your father, Martha, knew of her connections with August and was bitterly upset by her liaison with him, because her motives were so far removed from his own. Jeremiah was very young and quite passionate in his desire to help, but he was not altogether as discreet as a wiser more experienced person might have been. Marilor was passing information on and hoping to get the airmen caught and she assumed that my son was doing the same. August was very afraid that she would get him in to trouble and he had to be very careful of the information he gleaned. He even fed some of it to the Germans, knowing when there was no risk. He had very little to do with her after the birth of her first child. He recognised the potential for danger that she represented, not just to himself but to the resistance movement. He continued his alliance with her in order to prevent her taking up with anyone else, though I believe that was not in fact the case.' She stopped to sip her coffee, and then said,

'Calvin, would you fetch the photo from the hall please?' Calvin brought it back and gave it to her.

'This is me with August, just a few years before he went to War.' Gertrud handed the photo to Abigail. Abigail took her time, studying the photo and concentrating on keeping her emotions in control.

'I see. So my mother told the Priest the truth. I look like him don't I? How strange this all feels.' After another long and silent moment, she handed the photo to Martha, the only one who had not yet seen it. Martha studied the photo and gave a wry smile as she handed it back to Gertrud but turned instead to Abigail.

'I'm so sorry we are not sisters!'

'It makes no difference, Martha, I'm just so happy we met.'

'I can see you two get on well together, but I'm happy to have found you as well, another granddaughter.'

'I fear your grandson may not feel the same way. He was antagonistic towards the possibility that his father might have been unfaithful to his mother. Should we perhaps let him carry on believing that? '

Gertrud appeared to give this some thought.

'August didn't know you were his child. He knew she was close to Jeremiah, though he didn't know they were married. If he thought about it at all, I imagine Marilor would have let him believe Jeremiah was the father and after that, she let everyone think the child was her sisters'. I think she would change her story to suit whomever she was with. You may find this hard to believe, but until I saw you for the first time earlier, I didn't know either. This is just as much a shock to me as to you. Hans told me of your story about the Priest so I have had some time to think about it all. It's true that Hans carries a torch for his father, he hardly ever saw him and when he did, it was briefly and he was in uniform. An intimidating and powerful image to a child. His mother has been a constant burden to him, so he naturally idolised his father. He is quite bitter about the execution and this is why I've nurtured his feelings that his father was a brave man and not the cowardly traitor he was shot as. It would do no good for him to know that he was also unfaithful.'

'Your grandson mentioned Monsieur Rombouts? Was he really also to blame for his execution? We stayed with him for a few days in St-Pierre-Sur-Dives. He and his wife were very welcoming and we got on so well with them. It seems so unlikely.'

'Henri Rombouts. Yes, my son blamed him, didn't he? August told me about his poor wife, she was so often unwell. It left Henri with too much spare time I fear. He too fell under the spell of Marilor. Your mother must have been a siren in her day! You are very fortunate Abigail, to have inherited the good looks of both your parents! But after you were born and Marilor returned to St. Pierre-Sur-Dives, August discouraged her while still maintaining the contact because he recognised that she was dangerous. He no longer trusted her and now that Jeremiah had gone, her source of information was also weak and unreliable. My son also realised that she was having an affair with Henri, an upright and respected man in the community who was quite obviously patriotic. But the man had his weakness and August thought it was probably Henri's child she was carrying when she was arrested. He knew that it wasn't his as their intimacy had long since ceased.'

'It would have been 1945 by then, the end of the War and the start of recriminations and accusations which were building up at that time, bursting like a bubble from too much pressure built up from stresses and strains. Many people were euphoric in their rush to enjoy the newly won freedom, but constant worry followed by sudden release causes people to behave in all sorts of uncharacteristic ways, much as the War had brought out its own previously unimaginable behaviours.'

'Henri's wife was at last successfully carrying a child to full term and so Monsieur Rombouts was suddenly struck with a newly found conscience and was very afraid that his deceit with Marilor would come to light. In an effort to distract attention away from himself, he chose that moment to remember his patriotic duties and to point an accusing finger at her. Others, though not many I believe, attacked her as well and she was subsequently imprisoned as a traitor. Henri had taken on a temporary post as Mayor during the War years which gave him certain powers. August knew that Monsieur Rombouts had let it be known that August was the father of the child Marilor was carrying when she was arrested. By then, Philippe, Augusts' cousin had been captured and shot by the Germans. I heard this later from my sister-in-law. Happily her husband survived the War and they had another child, a daughter.'

'The War was over and so they allowed August to come home for some sort of trial and we had one last meeting. There were rumours by his fellow officers of his passing on information to the wrong quarters but it was his fraternisation with the enemy, Marilor, which was to be the final curtain for him and getting her pregnant was sufficient to have him sentenced to death. Ironically, as I have said, this second pregnancy was not the one of which he was guilty and the Trial was a farce, over in minutes. His defence was not listened to and he had no legal representation. Ironically, the Authorities had no proof of his involvement with Philippe because there was no-one left to interrogate. He so nearly succeeded in being completely undiscovered. So he was not shot as a traitor, as I led my son to believe, but for being unfaithful to his wife and unfaithful to the Aryan race. So yes, I'm sorry to tell you that Monsieur Henri Rombouts caused the death of my son, your father, a fact which he probably does not even know.' Abigail looked sympathetically at the young couple.

'I didn't know these people, the Rombouts. It was only their son Stefan who came to see me and he didn't have a very good relationship with his father.'

'I suppose people change? What do you think Calvin? Did he actually lie to us?' Martha asked him. 'He talked about the War and his duty. I suppose he just avoided telling us about his affair! Can you believe it was also him that made the accusations against Marilor?'

'Mon Dieu! That would mean he was instrumental in the death of BOTH of my parents! Is he some sort of monster?' Abigail said softly, the dawn of realisation causing her a look of horrified pain.

'It's War that is the monster. This man, Henri, he had a particular position to uphold. He felt it was his moral duty to tell what he knew and in fairness, he must have deliberately waited until after the War was over before telling all, because the deeds performed by Jeremiah were never revealed by him. I suspect he thought that both Marilor and August were traitors and were both equally guilty.'

'What about his moral duty to his wife? He was unfaithful to her.'

'Those morals must have come out of a different drawer!' She smiled at Martha's indignation.

'Perhaps guilt and jealousy made him want to rid himself of both of them. Who knows? Men do not always see themselves as unfaithful. Many men separate sex from love in their minds. Yet when sex and love and loyalty entwine together, you have a beautiful bond, a good marriage. And even sex alone can be like wine, light and sweet when you are young and inexperienced. But mix it with love and loyalty and it matures, and then one looks for quality and refinement. I don't excuse your Henri Rombouts, but he was himself young and immature, as were all the other players in this drama. I am sure that he and his wife are now far beyond where they were thirty five or forty years ago.'

'How can you be so forgiving?' Martha said.

'I'm too old to waste my energy on hatred, revenge, bitterness or blame. It won't bring them back. If you don't move on in your life, you're not living are you?' Not waiting for an answer, she carried on.

'We have been through a great deal, all of us. You two young people have travelled a long way to find out about the past, one which your father perhaps hoped you would discover after his death. It must have given you an insight into his true nature and what events moulded his character before you were even thought of. Not many people have that opportunity. I imagine it has also taught you a great deal about each other and maybe it has brought the two of you closer together. And Abigail, you had been fully accepting of your life as it had been told to you. Has the truth changed you? I doubt it; you seem such a rounded personality already. But it has brought you into my life, another child of my son. That is something I can treasure, every time I look at you and I hope that will be often and that you will become a frequent visitor. And me? I believe I have just found some new friends as well as family. I didn't know what to expect when I opened the door to you all this morning. But I'm glad I did and I am happy with what I have found. So now, a glass of wine I think and a toast to the future.'

Chapter 23

After they had drunk their toast it seemed a good time to take their leave. Telephone numbers and addresses were exchanged and Gertrud, who was now looking very tired, again expressed her pleasure and delight in their visit and waved them off at the front door after calling a taxi for them. Abigail said she had to get back to the hotel in Paris and would catch the afternoon train and Martha and Calvin agreed to meet her there that evening or if not, then the following day. They took the taxi directly back to the station and waved Abigail off before once again embarking on their journey to Paris.

They filled up with petrol and bought some bread, some sausage and some apples and planned their route to stop on the way at Rheims. They were setting off much later in the day than on their outward journey and thought they might have to stay overnight if they were too tired to continue. Martha was very aware that it was Calvin that had to do all the driving and she didn't want him to overstretch himself.

They made good time on the main roads, stopping once to eat their picnic lunch and arriving in Rheims in the late afternoon. As they had discovered before, the size of the lettering on their map denoting the town was no indication to its actual size and Rheims was larger than they had imagined. It was famous for champagne and so they bought a bottle to celebrate their success in finding Abigail, carefully stowing it away for later when they could share it with her. They cruised around the back streets and found a créperie that didn't look too busy and so they were able to order a *galette compléte avec frites* and eat it in what was for them a record beating time. They were well over half way to Paris so they were pleased to be able to arrive in Paris before dark.

The weather and the traffic continued to favour them and soon they were drawing up at the Hotel Campanile in Paris. The receptionist smiled in recognition and immediately put a call through to Abigail. She greeted them warmly, despite the few hours since seeing them and said she had not long been back herself. Calvin produced the champagne with a flourish and Abigail fetched the glasses, insisting they drank it straight away.

'A gift of wine should always be shared with those who give it, even if it's not quite chilled!' she said, then 'Santé!' they all echoed.

The three talked a little about their travels and then Calvin reminded them all that they should be planning their return to England. Martha knew he was right, they had their lives to pick up and jobs waiting for them.

'Abigail, could you perhaps take some leave and come to England? You could stay at my house, there are two spare bedrooms and I would so love to show you around. Or you could be free to do as you wish.'

'Thank you so much, I think I would like that very much. I've never been to England and I'm sure I could arrange for the time off. In the past, I have had holiday time and stayed in the hotel and then quite often I have been called to help out and ended up by not having a holiday at all! Of course, not all the time, you understand.'

'That's great! When can you come?'

'I think I'll need a couple of days to arrange something. Would that be all right? Perhaps we could travel on the ferry together?'

'Wonderful.'

Chapter 24

A light rain was falling, but they all agreed that the summer had been a good and revealing one when they all met again at the Ferry Terminal in Calais. The ferry trip was unremarkable and when they arrived in England they were met with the first signs of autumn cloaking the trees. The rain had followed them causing Calvin to ride slowly on the now greasy roads and so Martha had escorted Abigail to the train station in Dover and found her a connection to Maidstone. She had asked her to wait in Maidstone whilst they drove back to Elmswood where Martha could then collect her car to pick up Abigail from the station, leaving Calvin to unpack the motor bike, get some shopping and make up a bed for her.

Now that the immediacy had gone out of their quest, Martha was afraid that Abigail would be bored with her ordinary life. It bore no resemblance to the buzz of hotel life and she said as much to Abigail as they sat in the kitchen relaxing with their coffee. Her response was pragmatic as usual and reminded Martha very much of the similarity of character that existed between Abigail and Gertrud.

'Life is everything that you do. Hotels are places that people pass through and those people are anonymous to me. I don't know what their lives are really like and sadly I have no knowledge of family life either. Having a connection to people who I can say, 'I know that person,' is like having a family for me and I appreciate it. It means a lot to me and it's not boring.'

'You have a family now. All the Mennen family and us as well. So, speaking of living our life, tomorrow I would like to make some changes to the house, you know, decorate, change some of the furniture, that sort of thing. Will you help me? I'm pretty sure Dad kept some paint stored in the loft. Strange, I know, but I've never even been up there! '

'That would be fun; I've never done any decorating before! Shall we have a look and see what's up there now?'

'Great idea! Calvin could you fix the loft ladder for us? I don't know how it works and I don't want it to collapse with either of us on it!'

Calvin found the pole with a hook to pull it down but said he would then leave them to it. He wanted to visit his parents, collect his mail and get his clothes ready for work.

The two women, both nervous of the step ladder, took a torch with them to be able to find a hoped for light switch. This they found, a pull cord hanging from a cross beam and the room was instantly flooded with light. They were grateful not to have to change a bulb and also to discover that the attic floor had been boarded over. There was a small round window at one end, but it was insufficient to provide the necessary amount of light they would need to find anything. There were piles of books and old bits of furniture everywhere. They found a couple of ancient looking empty suitcases and stacked them on top of each other to make an impromptu seat. They perched together on it and looked around them. They spotted some cans of paint, two which had been started, one large pot of cream coloured emulsion, the other, a hue of green seldom seen on anything but old railway stations and which Martha could not recall having seen on anything before. There was a third tin with a rusty lid which looked as if it may have once contained varnish but which now sounded solid when they shook it.

'I suppose we could use the cream one, but it's not very inspiring is it?'

Abigail nodded. 'We could use it as a border or just on one wall and then choose a prettier colour for the rest of the room. Which room were you going to start with?'

'My bedroom, I think, because it has always been my room, sort of personal to me, if you know what I mean. I don't want to change everything that was here when my dad was alive. I suppose I just want to put my identity on a few things.'

'Good idea. What else is up here?'

Let's have a look shall we? There's a little writing desk over there in the corner, I think that must have been my Grandma's, you know, my dad's mum.'

Martha went to the little window where the desk stood and sat at the round stool which was tucked beneath it. The drawer under the writing area was locked but the key was easily discovered, attached by a piece of wool and tucked inside another small drawer, one of a pair on each side of the desk.

She unlocked the drawer and found that the small space inside was full to the edges with red note books. Each one had a year on the front in bold black numbers. The hand which had written inside the books was neat but childish and had her father's name written across the top of the first page. Picking one at random, she read aloud.

'*1932. I played cricket with Fred and Eric today and I scored 20 runs. Howzat!*' Look, here's another one. *Today was the saddest day of my life, because my father died. I have not cried for a long time, but today, I cried.* Oh that's so sad. He must have only been about eleven then. Here's another one. *Mum gave me a thick ear today, because I spent the change from the shopping on sweets.* Little monkey! My grandma was a lovely person, he must have deserved it.'

'You are so lucky to have known your family Martha. It's lovely to hear all this. Do you think there is one for 1939? Or 1936, the year he went to France?'

'Yes, here's one. Let's see, they're all over the place at the moment. *Mum has met a bloke. He seems all right but he won't replace my dad for me. I'm going to stay with Auntie Rose for a bit. Now that I can leave school I don't know what to do so I'm going to see what it's like doing fruit picking near Sittingbourne where she lives.* Oh and here's another bit. *I like Sittingbourne and I have got myself a job picking blackcurrants. It's a bit boring and the bosses are dead fussy but the people who do the fruit picking are a jolly crowd. Whole families live like gypsies but I don't mind because I'm going to save up for a bike. Aunty says the world is my oyster, but France sounds quite interesting.* Then here's another page . . . .

Aunty says I should let Mum and the new bloke have some time to themselves, so when I get my new bike I'm going to France. I've seen a Hercules in the bike shop, second hand for thirty bob. They're over 4 quid new. The man said I should get a puncture outfit and some spare brake blocks if I'm going far. He doesn't write every day but it's very neat. This is great!'

Abigail joined her at the desk, looking over her shoulder. 'What an interesting boy! I rather wish he HAD been my father. Lucky you and to find all this stuff too! Shall we take them downstairs and look at them in comfort? The lights not very good up here.'

'There's a different sort of notebook here, I reckon these might be the ones he wrote in France. Shall we take these as well?'

'Good idea. I'll fetch a bag or they'll be all over the place.'

Once they had carried the notebooks down the steps and put them in to some sort of order, Martha phoned Calvin and asked him to buy a Chinese take-away. She told him about the diaries and said she would put a couple of bottles of white wine in the freezer to chill them quickly. She knew he would be interested in the diaries and thought they could all browse through them together. An hour or so later, they were all set.

'You start Martha, he's your Dad.'

'OK. Here goes. I have just opened one at random. *The bike is marvellous and Uncle Pete gave me a rucksack to carry all my bits in. I rode it back to Mum's to test it and to thank her for the ten bob she gave me. The new bloke seems all right but she was a bit weepy when I told her I was going to France, but the bloke said she shouldn't namby pamby me so he's got my vote!* Then further on, he says: *Going for a long ride every day to get fit. Aunty says she can't afford to feed me and I should eat the fruit I pick. I don't think The Big Boss Man would agree!* Then on this next page he says, *France tomorrow! Uncle bought me a second hand French/English dictionary to take with me.*'

Calvin looked up from shuffling through the books, 'You've got to admire him, he's just a kid and he can't even speak the language. Look here, he's in France now. *I like the sound of the French voices and I'm surprised that they seem to understand me. Sometimes I just repeat back what they've said and they laugh and say something that sounds like san fay rien, which I think must mean it doesn't matter. I suppose it doesn't, either.* And then further on he says: *The land is very flat and doesn't change very much. Miles and miles of it and so far I have been sleeping in little bits of scrubby woods or under bushes near the side of the road as I couldn't find anywhere else and I was tired. Once I slept in a tiny barn that I found which is not much better but at least it kept me dry as it rained all day. I will look for a farm tomorrow because I'm running out of food.* Poor kid! Let's see what he does for money. Yes, here's something. *I tried to change some money in a shop today, but the man wouldn't take it. Instead he gave me some stale bread and showed me how to dip it in water to make it eatable. I think he was trying to tell me that milk is better, but at least the water's free! Maybe he didn't understand I wanted some French money instead of English, but he was kind and he gave me some apples too.* Wow! This kid's living rough!' said Calvin with admiration in his voice and Abigail and Martha both nodded their agreement.

'I don't think they would have wanted English money, after all, what could they have done with it?' said Abigail.

'Ah, well he must have found that out, listen to this. *Last night, before it got dark, I met some people cutting cabbages in a field. I offered to help by pointing at myself and then at the cabbages and they gave me a knife and showed me what to do. They asked me lots of questions so I just kept saying my name, pointing to the bike and saying Angleterre to them. They thought it was funny. When they stopped working,*

I pointed to myself and to them and did walking things with my fingers. They were really friendly, one man put his arm round my shoulder and picked up the bike and we all walked to his farm where a little old woman was cooking some stew. We all ate round the table and they gave me some very watery wine, but I didn't mind. I'm not used to wine. Then a bit later on he says*: I slept in the barn last night and I woke up suddenly when I felt the air whirring past my face. I was quite scared for a minute, because it was really eerie. Then I saw it was an owl, the most beautiful bird I have ever seen, it shone white and gold in the dawn light. I went outside and there were thousands of stars. I even saw one that shot across the sky like a meteor. I wonder if mum has ever seen stars like these.* That is so lovely, don't you think? What have you found, Abigail?'

'Well, it looks as though he slept in their barn for a few days until the cabbage crop was all gathered in and they fed him every day, then pointed him to the next village where they told him there were a few more farms. Probably the Piske's farm in St Pierre because he says, *I've fallen on my feet here, a man told me there was work to be found 10 minutes up the road and he was right because this old man says he could use a garçon, that's me because he hasn't got a wife, just two daughters. I'd better send a few postcards home now that I've got a job.* He usually just writes down the day and on this one he has started writing it in French, but you're right, there are lots of days when he doesn't write anything. It's hard to tell because he doesn't always write the whole date and some haven't got the year on the front.'

'This Chinese food is delicious, I've never had anything quite like it, thanks Calvin. They don't serve this sort of thing in any of the French Hotels I've worked in.'

'The wine's not bad either,' said Martha. Can I have a top up please? Mmm . . . things are progressing, listen to this: *Marilor came to my straw bed in the barn last night. I thought she had come to see the kittens but she said it was me she wanted. Then she asked me was I a virgin. I laughed. Well, I'm not anymore but I'm not telling her that! I think she'd done it before anyway.* Then a bit further on he says: *I met some of Marilor's friends last night and they taught me to play boules. It was jolly good fun and I think my French must be getting better because they don't laugh at me so much. I biked home in the dark and Marilor stayed at the cafe because she's got a job there now. Then I saw this enormous black pig with tusks. It made me jump and I nearly fell off my bike. I was really scared but I think he was too, because he ran into the woods squealing.* Wow, I bet that WAS scary. It must have been a wild boar. Hey look, there's a whole book here full of phrases and words he has learned. I think he must have checked the spelling from the dictionary but it's not bad, some of it is phonetic but even so, it's impressive. I'm trying to remember how I knew he was good at French; I think it was when I had homework, he was nearly always able to help me. Why did I never ask him how he knew? I doubt he learned any French at school.'

'That's life Mattie. No point in beating yourself up over it. Anyway, you're probably learning a whole lot more from reading these.' Calvin laughed and as usual his comment was protective and kind and Martha smiled acknowledging he had a point.

'You're right. You tend to think your parents' life starts when you're born and finishes when you leave home. And also that your identity is dependent on knowing who your parents are. How immature! That wasn't how it would have been for you Abigail. So how was it?'

'When I was very young, I don't remember being at the farm. Just some vague memories of my mother putting me in a box in the garden and telling Jean-Paul to watch over me. But to be honest, I don't really know whether it was Janice or Marilor. Then after I went to the Abbey, it was only Hervé who came to see me. I never called him 'papa' always Hervé and I suppose I must have been told to do that. I grew up with the idea that they were too poor to keep me and so I accepted that the Home was a better place for me to be. They kept us so busy there, we didn't have any spare time to think about our identity. We were united in our detachment from the rest of the world I suppose. We had no real entertainment other than listening to the nuns singing and playing the piano, from a distance, of course. So we ourselves sang. Different children knew different songs from their past lives and we all learned them. We did each other's hair, we skipped and ran, we recited poetry, and we drew pictures. I suppose what I'm saying is that we learned a certain independence and self reliance. We didn't have an acknowledged inheritance or identity so we grew to know ourselves by knowing each other. Probably also by how the other children behaved towards us. Children can be cruel and there were some tough kids there, but we all knew that they were not nice children and more to be pitied than hated. It really wasn't a bad life, you know, no worse than poor families living in the French countryside at that time, maybe better than some.'

'I still think you must have been a very sensible well balanced little girl, Abigail. You must have been born like it.' Still flicking pages, Martha carried on: 'Hey, listen to this. *Today, the Jewish woman called Hannah came to see me. I had been mending the boat I found as nobody seemed to know whose it was and then she told me she was scared, she said there are notices saying you must report to the police station if you are Jewish and she said she had never thought of herself as Jewish, she didn't follow the faith and her family had been French Roman Catholics for two generations. What should she do? Why did she ask me? She said she thought I could help her get away. Where to? I said, I don't know anywhere that would be any more safe than where you are. I told her to keep a low profile. What else could I do?* Oh my, this must have been the family Monsieur Rombouts told us about. How terribly sad. I'll see if I can find anything else about her. I can't tell how much later this is, it's several pages further on but he says: *I have just found out that Hannah was taken by the Germans a few days ago. They came for her at night and accused the family of harbouring a Jew, which is against the Law. The family denied it but the soldiers dragged her out of bed, barely giving her a chance to put on a coat and shoes. They left her husband and his family alone but shot the dogs. I cannot believe what difference the life of this poor woman could make to them. When I told Marilor, she looked at me strangely and said, she wasn't one of us.* That's terrible. She must have been tough as old boots! Sorry Abigail.'

'No, you're right. When you spoke earlier of family identity, perhaps it is good that she did not bring me up. I would not like to be so hard, like she evidently was.'

'Listen to this.' Calvin started to read. *'Today I found a British airman! He was curled up in a hedge and he was very frightened and obviously injured. He was very surprised when I spoke to him in English and wanted to know what I was doing here. I told him all about where I was from and then I said, what about you? He said he had joined the RAF because he had been a cadet at a posh school I had never heard of, but he said that was why he was a pilot. He was only a couple of years older than me. He said his plane had been shot at by a German. His engine had caught fire and he had to bail out. He said it was very frightening because he could hear the plane behind him screaming down in its last dive and that he felt weird because both he and the aircraft were completely out of control. He twisted his ankle badly on a big piece of granite when he landed and now he could hardly walk. I helped him to a better hiding place, a small quarried area where bits of old machinery had been dumped. Plenty of cover for him and then I went back to the farm. No-one was in so I took some eggs from the chicken run and boiled them up for him and picked some lettuce as well. I didn't risk taking any brea because it would have been missed. Then I went to see Claude and he told me whereabouts on the river I could take my English friend and that I should go tonight. Paul, the English pilot was still there on my return and I told him about the boat I had mended and that I would take him to a rendez-vous later that night. He was so grateful, it made me feel good to be able to do something to help. When I go back to England, I think I'll join the RAF, it sounds very exciting. Paul said there are lots of things I could do apart from flying, but I wouldn't mind that either.* Wow, that's how he got interested in the Airforce I guess. Here's another bit. *At supper today, Old man Piske said he had heard about Hannah the Jewish woman and that people were saying it was Marilor who had told the Germans. He asked her outright if it was true. She is scared of him and said no it wasn't. But I saw her eyes. Please God, say it wasn't her, because it was me who told her about Hannah in the first place. I am sick with the worry of it all.* There's more. *I don't feel married. Marilor is not a wife to me and she has changed. She taunts me for being young, for being British, for hating the Germans who she says have always been their friends and will be again when they have won the War. Somehow, I still manage to save an airman or two or at least help them on their way. I was told that there is someone in the German camp who is on our side, I don't know who it is. How ironic it would be if it was that handsome jerk August.*

This one is 1941. *The birth of Marilor's child is not far off. Although I am an innocent in these matters, I believe it should be closer than it appears to be. It is not mine, of that I am certain now and she has admitted as much. Last week, one of the Canadian airmen was found shot in the head and just left to rot. Erique and I and two others buried him in the woods and I took his tags. I shall return them to his unit when I get back to England. Not long now. The airman was due to meet me here and I was to take him down river to meet the others. I shall miss this life, but I am sure another awaits me in England and it will be good to see my mother again. She won't recognise me!* This is so sad. How long he goes on writing for?'

Calvin picked up a notebook which looked more tattered than the others and started to read. '*How strange it feels to be in England and it is ages since I wrote in this book. There are so many more people here and the silence has a different quality, more secretive and brooding. In France, you felt the fear but you could get away from it. My bicycle trip to the beach was frightening but I was more hungry than afraid. Once, a German stopped me and asked where I got the bike from. I told him I had stolen it and he laughed, but he took me for French. I ate fruit and raw vegetables and slept under hedges, but I had lost my bedroll and it was cold at night. When I got to the coast, I had to leave my bike, there wasn't enough space for it on the boat. It was rough on the Channel and there were several of us, all English. I felt ill all the way and didn't get to know anything about the others because they were sick too. So with no bike, I had to walk to Maidstone. To set myself up, the first thing I did was to go into a public Gents and have a wash, then I bought a dinner with my English money, which I had kept all this time because I hadn't been able to use it in France. It was great! Real gravy! I didn't really know the way to go home, so I went down the coast a way, because it was quite pleasant weather and then followed the signs to Canterbury. It took me two days because I just kept at it, but my shoes are not the best! I saw bomb damage and bomb shelters, it is grim. In France there was always talk about activity around the Ardennes and also at the Maginot Line, the fortification of the Swiss and Belgian borders. No-one seemed to know much detail about what was going on here. To happier things, today I saw my Mum. She seems well enough and contented with her life with Bert. To me she looks quite old, but it has been four years. I think she was shocked at my appearance as well but I too am older. She said how thin I was and started fussing immediately. But now that I am old enough, this week I shall go and recruit with the RAF.'*

Martha was looking over Calvin's shoulder and turned the page in the book. It was written in ink where all the other entries had been in pencil and sensing some significance in this, she read it out.

'The War is ended and how grateful I am that it's all over. But my heart is heavy with the news from France. Jean-Claude, my friend from the cafe has told me of the death of Hugo, my brave asthmatic friend. He died of a severe attack which took him before he could be given oxygen. Jean-Claude also told me that Marilor had been led through the streets in shame as a traitor. It made me so sad. He sent me the birth certificate of the child, Abigail, who bears my name but she isn't mine. He told me that she is cared for by Janine and

Hervé as if she was their own. I am glad of that. Then he starts a new page:

MY WAR. America has joined the War and now, so have I! I was sent to RAF Benson in Oxfordshire and after the initial training I was selected to fly in one of the converted Spitfires doing what they called 'aerial intelligence.' I started in a PR Mk 1X then progressed to a PR Mk X1, with extra wing mounted fuel tanks so that we could stay out for longer and we used universal camera installation, as they were easier to change instead of the front and rear mounted cameras that were on the 1X. All very modern and things have come a long way since we first started spying on Germany in the late '30's.

It was a strange feeling, skirting around France to fly over Germany. We were shot at so many times it's a wonder I am still here. Some of the Reconnaissance planes were armed, but not ours and we were constantly targeted, flying so low. I relied totally on the pilot and got used to looking the other way when we were under threat. There was nothing I could have done so I concentrated on developing a thick skin and taking my notes and observations. I made up a sort of shorthand and then if I was late taking the picture, I sketched what I saw instead, detailing whether it was to be a possible target or had been a successful hit. Then I had to unfathom my notes on our return! From up there, I could see just how much damage we had done to each other and now that it's all over, I wonder if things will ever be the same again.

I have been offered a secret spy post in the RAF, which I have declined. My years in France involving so much intrigue and secrecy have left me feeling weary of it all. But I have signed up for a further 10 years with the RAF and I will re-train as a draughtsman. It will put me in a good position to return to a normal life, when I shall put all this behind me forever.

Chapter 25

Martha's Diary

It's May 2011 and we have come here to St. Pierre-Sur-Dives to celebrate Abigail's 70th birthday. We bought a house in France some years ago now and I love being here for weekends and holidays, but of course today is special. We hired a hall that caters for weddings and parties of all kinds near to this beautiful old town. The weather was kind to us and we had canapés on the lawn with sweet white wine or cider to choose from. The tables inside were set with huge cauldrons of bœuf bourguignon and serving dishes filled with waxy white potatoes and glazed herb coated carrots and we all helped ourselves. There was vegetable lasagne for the non meat eaters and the children liked that as well. We had cheese, then gateaux and then the calvados bottle went up and down the tables, drunk neat or added to coffee after the wine had all gone.

Yes, 'we' is Calvin and me. After that unforgettable year in 1980 I decided I couldn't live without Calvin and happily, he felt the same way. He is kind and sweet and funny and he looks after me. After our 'Voyage of Discovery' as we liked to call it afterwards, we settled back into our respective lives for a week or two, catching up with everything and getting to know Abigail a little better. It was wonderful that she was there with us to share the diaries! Then one evening, Calvin came round to see me and said he couldn't settle back to how things were before we went away together. I felt the same, but I had tried to put it down to the newness of all the experiences and people we had met. I suppose I was still a bit afraid to commit to another emotion while everything was still a bit topsy turvy in my head. Well, my darling Calvin wasn't, he knew exactly what he wanted! He suggested that he moved in while I thought about it. So cheeky! I loved it! So that's what he did. The neighbours had to find something else to talk about after that. Calvin's' parents were great and so warm and welcoming and to everyone's delight, his old Jamaican grandma came to our wedding, dressed in the most amazingly colourful dress. She was a great attraction and nearly stole the show. So now we have two children, a boy called Grant and a girl called Mathilda. They inherited Calvin's lovely brown skin and my dark hair and of course they are both grown up now. We all went to Jamaica a few years back and met cousins and great aunts and uncles. They made us so welcome, passing us around to stay with one family after another, feeding us exciting food, singing to us and acting like we were celebrities. I am so proud of being part of his family and now having our own children and two little grandchildren as well, Ellie and Sophie from my daughter. They are gorgeous and spent the whole time at the party running around outside and playing with the various visiting dogs and children.

Monsieur and Madame Rombouts both died within six months of each other in 1991 but I would not have invited them anyway. We didn't contact them again directly other than to send the occasional card and to tell them that we had found Abigail. We had said we would call in on our way back but I couldn't face them after what we had leaned. Gertrud Mennen was such a queen of philosophy, that although we took her way of thinking about him to heart, I personally couldn't bring myself to feel the same way about Monsieur Rombouts ever again. I knew that if I saw him, I would be thinking about Marilor and not that lovely relaxed time we had with them both. I wanted to conserve those nice memories in aspic, if you know what I mean. In any case, it was Abigail who had unknowingly been affected the most by his actions and she had never met him as an adult. After hearing about his part in the life and death of both her parents, she didn't want to see him either. Can you blame her! She has a pretty good relationship with Hans and his family who are, I believe well aware that she is Hans' half sister but he still cannot bring himself to acknowledge her outright. Keep up with the Counselling Hans! We laugh about it now, his awful mother and his pompous ways. He is here too with Maria and their three children who we finally met at the funeral of Gertrud Mennen. She died in 1985 and Abigail, who had kept in touch with her quite closely in those last five years of her life, was very, very sad. They had formed a real bond and she often went to see her. Gertrud would reminisce about the old days when she was a dancer, or talk about August when he was a small boy. It was quite strange, she understood that Abigail obviously had quite a few large gaps in her upbringing as far as family memories went and Gertrud was intent upon filling them with nice things. No more talk of war or traitors, she even told her about ex boyfriends as well as all about Karl. I don't think she had ever been able to talk to Hans or Maria like it, probably because they were always so busy. And Abigail liked having a human being who loved her unconditionally, and Gertrud, in her frail old age, was happy to be looked after and for her affairs to be so skilfully organised. Han's mother also died that year from a stroke. She lingered on for a few weeks but the stroke was pretty severe and she lost the will to live and died in her sleep. After all the sorting out from two deaths in the family within months of each other, I think Hans and Maria finally learned the value of living for the moment and relaxing into their own skins. They are quite happy and chilled these days and they appreciated the role Abigail took in Gertrud's life having looked after his mother for so long with no other support. All his grandchildren from his sons and daughter still treat the place like home in between University and job training and they all love it. Hans had counselling after his mother died and I think that gave him the idea to expand the sports therapy business to include a clinic for psycho-therapy. A very good and profitable idea as the two can often be linked, especially these days when sport is taken so seriously. The house is so big and of course, he owns it all now and draws a very comfortable income from the Clinic to supplement his old age pension. I think he must be seventy five or thereabouts.

Stefan was also here, with Nathalie and their two children who of course also aren't children anymore and have children of their own. The little ones sat on the wooden square of the dance floor playing with building blocks and then knocking them down. Michel was there too with his gorgeous Parisian wife, so typical of Michel to have a gorgeous wife! They had no children, quite obviously from choice and they enjoy a very pleasantly sophisticated cosmopolitan life style. I think his legal practice must have gone from strength to strength after he moved it to Paris!

I'm so pleased the party went well. Abigail wasn't by herself; she had her latest man friend with her, a guy called Josef who is really sweet. She never married, she became more and more of a career woman in the hotel business and she is never short of a partner when we see her. Even though we are not related, it's the most wonderful thing, we are like sisters despite the fifteen years difference in our ages. I love Abigail, she is an extra grandmother to my family and we see her a lot. It may be because we are both a bit short on family members that we turned to each other but I don't think it's just that. It's as if that whole adventure was meant for us to meet whether or not we were related. I'm so glad we did.